The Ice Forest

Michael McGuire

The Ice Forest

The Marlboro Press
Marlboro, Vermont

First edition

The publication of the present volume has been made possible by a grant from the National Endowment for the Arts.

Manufactured in the United States of America

Library of Congress Catalog Card Number 90-60883

ISBN 0-910395-59-4

Two of the stories included in this collection have appeared previously: "A Winter Death" was first printed in *New Directions in Prose and Poetry (ND44)*, copyright © 1982 by Michael McGuire; and "The Shadow of the Mountain" in *The Hudson Review*, Fall 1978, copyright © 1978 by Michael McGuire.

THE MARLBORO PRESS

MARLBORO, VERMONT

For Catherine

Contents

The Ice Forest

A Winter Death

A friend of a former client met at a cocktail party had invited the lawyer up here. And, for some reason, perhaps because he was a little at a loss after winding up his practice, on the spur of the moment (unusual for him) he had accepted and decided to come up for the weekend. The client's friend was an artist, and above the fine hardwood floors of his house, his original works covered the walls. Also present were a friend of the artist, who was a potter, and the potter's wife and the artist's wife. The still young wives had known each other before (in fact, this was the reason for the continued association of the couples); oddly enough, they had once danced together in scanty, sequined outfits, with feathers covering their breasts, and pink hearts, like valentines, concealing their vaginas; they had been oggled together by drunken businessmen, and together they had mugged and aped the corny sight gags that insured their return engagements. These facts had been revealed to the lawyer, and not *sotto voce*, by the potter's wife.

Now the two women sat quietly talking in the artist's winter vacation home. Beyond the double plate-glass windows snow fell silently. The artist's wife's young daughter practiced her *grands battements* at the *barre* in tiny black tights. Her small swinging foot scuffed the floor regularly, like a pendulum that would not be still. Occasionally she

1

looked at herself, almost blankly, in the floor-length mirror. And, from time to time, her mother looked at her.

It was a late Sunday morning. The three men sat in soft widely separated chairs by the empty fireplace. Though the central heat was on, the huge stones of the fireplace looked cold and the smell of last night's blaze was still strong in the air. The floor around them was littered with discarded magazines and toys, and the inner surface of the immense windows was gray with cigarette smoke. Later in the day, after a walk together upon the cold, inhospitable beach—which always seemed at this time of year, the artist said, to want to be alone—they would go their separate ways. From his seat the lawyer could see the artist's picture of his wife: small and dark, hanging unevenly between the kitchen and the hall, not much more than a scribble in never-finished charcoal, as if the artist had tried, tried hard to complete it, but had somehow not been able to. Yet it was her.

"Look at these hands," said the artist, spreading his large-knuckled, almost oversize hands for all to see. "Meant for working the land, you think? Perhaps there really is peasant blood back there, but sculpture was my love. My love," he repeated. "Yet somehow, after I began to teach, there was never time. And that was twenty years ago. Even if I were . . . to go back . . . I wonder if I could lift the hammer or even hold the chisel now." He paused and looked around him. "Now I look at my land, I watch my children grow; we cut our Christmas tree together . . ."

The potter and the lawyer looked at the tree: huge for its purpose, now more or less denuded, dried out and shedding profusely, it lay on its side by the door ready to be dragged outside again and burnt in the spring.

"You sure you found that tree on your land?" inquired the

potter shrewdly. "I noticed a nasty-looking stump on the walk over here—well within my acres."

"I'll show you the spot," laughed the artist. "It was a hell of a trek dragging that tree, even with all of us pulling."

As they bantered the lawyer's mind wandered to the night before when, content just to be there in a new environment, at a little distance, listening to the voices, he had sat close to the roaring fire, his drink cradled in his hand, and separating herself from the smoke and the murmur, the artist's wife had seemed to materialize close at hand and sat down next to him. He acknowledged her presence, and then his eyes returned to the fire. They sat some time without speaking. Now and then her youngest daughter would sidle up to have her mouth wiped or to raise her shirt and display her tiny, swelling belly as if she, in her turn, were already heavy with another, smaller version of herself. And in the moments of relative solitude, the artist's wife had seemed to be talking to him alone, and he (an older man?) had been content to listen.

"I took a year off once," she said, "from everything. It wasn't that long ago. I lived in a hole in dirty, gray New York. I never made a meal. I'd eat standing up, the bag from the grocery store on the counter right beside me. But I was alone!" she said, leaning closer, her voice thick with relief. "Do you know what that is: not even a dog or a sleeping child; no door opening, no sound of feet coming toward you, no . . . breathing? I hesitate to call myself anything," she added quietly, looking more into the fire than at him, "but I do paint. And that was the year of the seven-foot canvases." She had paused. "Now I teach. We all teach. There is a very business-like atmosphere in the classroom. I teach the technology of it. The word 'art' never crosses my lips. I have tenure," she had said, looking more than ever like her portrait.

Now the men's conversation was over. Now it was time to drive down for a final walk along the beach. And the artist and his wife, and the potter and his wife, and the lawyer walked along the beach. This time it was colder than the woods, the north wind blowing down from the east-facing, deserted stretch of sand, and the sun was already out of sight behind the trees to the southwest. But though the landward view was dark, cold-looking, the sea was bright and alive and indifferent to the discomfort of the walkers, and its light graceful motion actively reflected the fast-fading, deep cerulean blue above it.

As they walked northward into the wind along the great flat expanse, tears were forced to their eyes, and at times they seemed to be blown apart, leaving each alone for a while with his own body and the cold, and then to come together again. A gull cried overhead. In the distance an old reddish coaster or fishing boat seemed to be moving aimlessly up and down, making little, if any, progress on a sea of azure brightness. More or less pointed toward the land, it never reached it while they were there, and moving at different speeds themselves, they were soon well-separated specks on the already colorless extent of sand.

The artist and the lawyer, struggling far in front of the others, and neither ready to admit that his heart was hammering, his breath short, and his face and hands nearly frozen, at length came to a stop together and turned downwind to relieve themselves. Even that operation was difficult with numb fingers, but a chill went out of the shoulder blades with the released pressure, and a reassuring steam was briefly visible.

"Tell me," asked the artist manfully, "what do you see when you look out across this land?"

The lawyer raised his eyes and saw several moving forms, central among them the artist's wife, the configuration that

4

TMP

THE MARLBORO PRESS

P.O. BOX 157

MARLBORO, VERMONT 05344

The Marlboro Press is an independent publisher of serious literature: works of fiction, of intellectual history and philosophic travel, biography, chronicles, essays—a good many of them in translation.

If you have found this book of particular interest you may wish to know what others have appeared on our list and are forthcoming. We will be happy to send you a catalogue, and to answer any queries you may have.

Name

Street or box number

City

State   Zip

had got her her first job noticeable even at this distance, her lovely girl children moving away from her and back to her as if they were on rubber bands.

"When I first stood here," continued the artist, "when I first saw the winter clouds reflected on the flat wet sand, I knew I had never seen anything like it, that I never would again. But there is no adequate response. When I stand here again after I've been away, I can't believe it was ever like this or, at least, that I had ever seen it. This must be some land I'm not supposed to enter."

Suddenly the wind dropped and the sound of voices carried to them across the sand. And for a moment the lawyer thought he heard the artist's wife laughing. He had never heard her laugh before, and his eyes opened a little wider at the sound. It may have been a bird flying somewhere out of sight, but at that distance, before the wind returned, he was just able to convince himself that he had truly heard her laughter, and even seen her laughing face.

Now, in silent agreement, the two men began to let the wind push them down the beach toward the scattered figures, the car, the women and children growing in the distance. "I know," the artist was saying. "You're tired of the smoke in your lungs, or the sound of feet and the mumble of massed voices. Well, you're perfectly welcome to stay, I mean in this part of the country, if you can find a place. See what you think of it after we've flocked back to our institutions, and you're left alone with the people who sell the groceries and pump the gas and fill the holes in the roads and put the telephone lines back up after a storm. See what you think."

In time the lawyer, perhaps for the second time in his life following an impulse, did learn what it was like to be alone there. The holidays over, his hosts had gone back to their classrooms, and he had found a room for rent with an old couple right on the sea. The room was upstairs and not very large, and the fact that he had seemed to have to step into part of the roof to look out his gabled window made it all the more picturesque. His face pressed near to the cold glass at an angle, for his room was on the side of the house and did not face the sea directly, he was able to look down through the boatyard, with its huge, sleeping hulks braced up with beams and covered with tarpaulins, and into the small, now freezing cold harbor. In a way, he had never been younger: he felt like the boy he had never been, not doing something he was supposed to, who could spend his evening making model ships if he wanted to—and who would ever know?

The couple were inoffensive enough; their only vice was television, but this was an all-consuming one. It didn't seem to matter what was playing as long as there was sound, motion, and the low, persistent buzz of the thing itself. Often, stopping in the doorway to the old-fashioned sitting room to conclude some small matter, the lawyer would make some friendly comment on the entertainment, only to have Mr. and Mrs. turn, somewhat surprised, to face their own machinery, obviously having had no idea of what was on it. And, no doubt, this little weakness had affected more than their minds: the bodies, left to themselves, had not hesitated to gather flesh; all those exciting daytime gifts of stoves, refrigerators, and freezers required some serious snacking—and of the most instantaneous "foods."

Over the mantelpiece stood their wedding photo, dated and discolored in a silver frame: he is a powerful young man with ambition in his eye; she is thin as a girl. There was another picture of them years later, already middle-aged, standing in what must have been the boatyard beneath the window: it is a summer's day, the boats are in the water—all except one, *Mon*

Rêve, which stands braced up on the skids waiting to be launched. Mr., dressed for the occasion, stands with one hand on her hull; Mrs., still thin, is ready with the bottle of champagne in her hand.

He had often meant to ask if the boat was still down there, up on the cement under one of the canvases, but it hardly seemed possible, and he didn't want to bring up any unpleasant memories. At night, after a few friendly words, the lawyer would excuse himself and go upstairs to pull on two pairs of socks and his insulated boots before stepping out for his night walk. This, too, might be considered the indulgence of a youthful whim: he had never in his life found time to dress up like a woodsman and tromp along listening to his feet breaking through the snow. And these were, perhaps, the best times, the times when he felt most like staying on and on. The cold bit into him the moment he closed the door behind him. Used to buttoning up as he hurried down the street in the city, he now learned to close positively every gap in his clothing and have both gloves on before opening the door.

Then his boots would sound, hard and adequate, on the bitterly cold bricks of the still street and on the even more desolate cement of the quay. There were one or two boats still floating in the small dark harbor, from time to time halfheartedly pulling their slime-covered chains and cables out of the water only to lower them again. Like neglected animals, under a winter sky clearly holding a million stars, they seemed to know how little they counted for in the scheme of things.

The lawyer's usual route, and he seldom varied it, was once round the harbor (by the light of the moon with luck, otherwise tripping now and then on lines and odd things made of metal and wood, which somehow seemed to change their places each night) and then up the steep, rocky path to the headland, which did not jut as far into the dark sea as the next one, and therefore did not boast the light intermittently visible in the distance: one long flash followed by a still longer period of darkness. Beneath him the small harbor was obscure and dreamlike. He could just see the little house and the window of his rented room, and he wondered what it would be like, a few years later, remembering this scene. Would it be strange, touched with emotions he couldn't quite place, like memories of childhood? Would he, in fact, dream about it? Or would he ask himself why, why in the world he had ever spent so many nights here?

After his not really so late "midnight walk," the routine was always the same: home by the same route, out of the double socks and the long johns, into the bed. Then, by a small bedside lamp, its shade tilted up, he would read the old, worn-out books that had seemed to be waiting for him all these years and that he had discovered stuffed into a carton underneath the angle of the roof: adventures of the seas and of the woods, of whaling and of trapping, and even a book of poems, a young man's poems, the occasional line of which he would ponder at length in his head. And before he turned the light out, it felt to him as if not just the household and the port but the entire world was sleeping peacefully. In the darkness the cold seemed to tighten its grip on the house, forcing all sorts of unidentifiable sounds from the old structure, but beneath the heaped covers he was safe as a child. And in the morning he sometimes managed a walk to the point of land before breakfast, sometimes in time to see the sun rising out of the sea.

Weeks passed. Of the few people around, none seemed interested in him, and he, on his part, did not venture to speak with anyone. What a change it was from the social contacts and obligations he had known. And yet, strangely enough perhaps, he experienced no restlessness or even loneliness. A

8

necessary time of silence he began to consider it and thought of the earth resting underneath the snow. Yet March came with its winds and changeable weather, and still he had no urge to go. At times he puzzled over this fact; he knew he did not have centuries ahead of him like the fallow land.

And he began to wonder why, really, he had come, and why he stayed on. Without many articles of faith, it had always seemed to him, in retrospect, that everything had had to happen just as it did. Now something in him had changed. He was aware of that. But why, and for what? At times he would think of working, of keeping up his contacts and holding onto his clients after all. Then he would sit down at the tiny, almost child-size desk in his room, arrange the blank paper neatly before him, and hold a full pen over it. But he could not bring himself to cross off the old address of his printed letterhead and write in his new, temporary one.

Then he would close all in his desk drawer and walk, and as he walked, always trying to extend his range by ever so little, it might occur to him to take up some cause before it was too late, to devote his energies. But just the thought of returning to the airless courtroom would leave him with a faint nausea. And occasionally, walking on the long, deserted beach where he and the artist had first left their footprints, he would become aware of how keenly he looked into the clear distance through the cold, salt air, as if he were on the lookout for a beached whale or the rockets from a dramatically wrecked ship. But there was only the recurring, variable weather and now familiar pattern of nights and days.

And, as the cold seemed gradually to release its grip, he found he could walk further and further each day until he was covering ten miles. What would his fellow New Yorkers say to that? And instead of hard gray pavement, he had the changing earth to walk upon; and instead of weak, unwilling legs, tired in a block, his legs swung out easily from his hips mile after mile: he found he had increased his stride and found a rhythm in walking which he fell into as soon as he left the house and started down the beach. Days passed, and the miles he had never covered before fell one by one behind him.

One day, on which the sun seemed to be seriously beginning to reassert itself, he followed the winding road out to the artist's house, perhaps simply because it was a destination, a goal. After a few miles further than he was used to, and at least one wrong turn, he came to a stop before it on healthily tired legs. The house confronted him, shuttered and deserted looking, its weathered wood almost the color of the cold muddy forest floor. There had been a steady rise in the land from the sea to the house, and he stood a moment, realizing how much further he really had come than he was used to. A dark cloud slid across the sun and, at the same time, a chill wind rustled through the trees which still held a few of last year's darkened, brittle leaves. He shivered involuntarily, and an unfastened shutter on the "old-fashioned" side of the house banged desolately.

Walking up to the house to fix it, he thought he could smell the damp ashes of an extinguished fire, and at the uncovered window he took the liberty of cupping his hands against the glass and looking in. His heart nearly stopped: only inches from his own an expressionless face seemed to be looking right through him. He started back, half aware of a look of shock and horror on his own face, and only as a reflection of sky and branches returned to the glass did he recognize, almost as an afterthought, the artist's wife. Partially recovering himself, yet still somehow apprehensive, he knocked, almost absurdly he felt, on the door, knowing there could be no answer. And, after a moment, he tried it, and finding it open, stepped in and shut the door behind him.

10

With only the occasional half-light from the single, unfastened shutter, it was necessary to stand a moment before proceeding. There was an airless, soundless quality to the semidarkness, and the penetrating cold was that of a deserted house. His footsteps sounded almost too slow, too casual as he advanced into the main room: the sound of a returning criminal, he thought for no reason, of a criminal returning to the scene of a crime which he had no reason to fear would ever be discovered and for which no alibi would ever be necessary. There was no telling how long the fire had been out; there was no wood; the artist's wife sat in a straight-backed chair before the empty fireplace. She had wrapped a blanket around herself; there was an empty cigarette pack and a glassful of ashes on the floor beside her.

The shutter banged open, and he noticed the rest of the furniture lined against the walls and covered with sheets. Somehow unwilling to approach the artist's wife directly, he walked around in front of her. Moving through the still air of the house, it seemed colder than outside. Her body hidden beneath the blanket, she seemed without form or shape. She did not look at him when he stood in front of her, and it occurred to him that, if she were to look up suddenly, his hair might stand on end.

"I didn't think there was anyone here," he said.

The shutter almost closed, then didn't and again banged open against the wall.

Without looking at him she exhaled briefly, as though she had thought of laughing at something to herself, but her laugh had gotten no further than that.

"Maybe there isn't," she said suddenly and without looking at him, the words seeming hardly to leave her lips.

All at once, and for no reason, he was angry.

"You're a young woman," he said abruptly.

11

She looked at him then, almost as if she were showing him that there was nothing at all in her eyes.

"What are you doing to yourself?" he said, too loudly. "What's happened?"

His words echoed meaninglessly. For a moment she seemed to see him, then he felt the vision of himself fading from her eyes. He waited, looking at her, imagining events a lawyer might be equipped to deal with. A minute passed, and then another. He had the feeling she would not object no matter how long he stood there looking at her. Her motionless face was, at that moment, a perfect picture of herself, the kind you come to a stop before and don't leave without looking back at several times. He felt himself hesitating between alternatives, but when he did walk away from her she did not turn her head. And outside, looking at the road, it occurred to him just to forget he had found anyone here and to go back the way he had come. Instead he found the ax and split some logs and came back and started a fire in the big fireplace. She had not changed her position when he returned. She neither moved nor watched him as he built the fire.

He learned quickly enough that there was no power in the house and no way of cooking except in the fireplace, where he managed to hang a kettle, peasant fashion, on a chain over the open flames. The fire was beginning to give some heat, and she seemed, in a somewhat puzzled way, to be looking at it. While the water was heating he went back outside and repaired the shutter. The wind had continued to blow, and one cloud had followed another across the low gray sky. It seemed to him, looking up, that the day had disappeared somewhere, morning proceeding directly into night. He fastened several other shutters open and returned to the somewhat lightened house just as the big kettle was beginning to steam and spit. Lifting it off the chain with a rag, he carried it to the kitchen where he located the tea and the pot. He discovered a tin of milk and an old box of sugar cubes in a cabinet and added enough of each to a cup to give her some strength. When he returned, he found her holding out her hands to the fire.

"Here." He handed her the tea.

She stared at it a moment, then slowly took it. He went back to the kitchen and poured himself a cup, then carried the kettle back in and set it near the fire, where it would stay warm. Not bothering to take the sheet off one of the large chairs, he shoved it nearer the fire and, making no attempt to move her, sat in it himself. After a moment he looked at her. She held the full cup with both hands wrapped around it, her elbows and knees close together as she hunched toward the flames. It seemed a long time before she tasted it again, this time looking down at it. She said something, but it was spoken too softly for him to hear what it was, and he didn't want to ask her to repeat it.

The rectangles of the windows began to darken. Now and then a fitful cold wind made a circle of the house, as if trying to find a way in. No one drove up the road or down it, for the season was neither one thing nor the other and the houses were without function and empty. He must have drowsed off briefly, not knowing how tired he really was. When he opened his eyes the fire had gone down and she was on her knees in front of it, carefully and silently rebuilding it. Aware of an unaccustomed lassitude in his body, he made no move to help her and simply watched. When the fire was blazing again, she went back to her chair.

Again they sat without speaking. With her hands lightly clasped in her lap, she seemed to be almost philosophically observing each flare-up and collapse in the structure of burning wood. Later, as the walls darkened and the wind again circled the house, flinging itself now at the door, now at the windows, it was his turn to rebuild and rekindle. Then he too returned to his chair. A lifetime might have passed since he started out from his room by the sea. But no one would miss him or come looking for him, any more than anyone from the city had. And what did it matter? Silence moved through his body like the warmth from the fire. Everything that had ever happened to him had happened so long ago it was difficult to remember a single incident, a single face. It seemed that he might have been married to this woman since she had come of age, might have known her a thousand times, and with the strong, never fully given love in him have kept this night forever at bay.

He woke to find the windows on one side of the house already light, the sky beyond them silvery gray. He looked at his watch without moving. Dawn. He did not remember falling asleep, but the sleep before dawn was always best, magical and full of dreams, as if already touched by the sun, still just out of sight and moving toward him. His face against the back of the chair, he found himself already missing the new routine of his nights and days, his attic room, and the still sleeping port. Perhaps now it was time to head quietly back down to the sea: once round the port, to the point of land—then in to breakfast. His hand moving down his side in preparation for rising encountered something unfamiliar, held it, and lifted it. He looked down. He saw in one glance that the blanket was on him and that her chair was empty.

He stood up slowly, feeling the stiffness in his legs, and folded the still warm blanket. It seemed so much a part of her that he was just tempted to sniff it primitively, but he set the folded blanket on the chair. The fire had only recently gone out, and the room was still warm. Not finding the artist's wife in the kitchen and expecting her to appear eventually from the bathroom, he stepped outside himself only to be surprised by the unseasonable return of winter: hard, driven flakes rushed

14

past the house. Already several inches of snow on the ground were staring back at a low, dark sky. After standing a moment behind a tree, he went back inside. He stood by the fireplace for several minutes, as though waiting at the spot where he had last seen her was sure to bring her out. There was not the faintest sound within the house, and the wind seemed to be whirling almost victoriously around it.

It took him only a second to step into the tiny hallway and observe the empty bathroom and two small, empty bedrooms, their flat, striped mattresses uncovered from Christmas to summer. He stepped once more into the kitchen, walking more quickly now, his body seeming to know by itself that it could move as it pleased, and his boots sounded loudly in the empty house. There was no one in the kitchen, of course, only a washed glass upside down drying in the sink.

Closing his coat carefully about him and pulling his hat down over his ears, he went outside again. This time he felt the door lock behind him when he closed it, and standing there on the snow-covered step, this time looking for signs or evidence, he at once saw what he had not noticed before: her small, light footprints leading to the road. Apparently she had gone soon after it had begun to snow: there were only the slightest indentations in the smooth, white surface, as if only her spirit had walked there. He followed the footprints out to the road. A highway department or telephone company truck, or both, had passed. On the road there was no way of knowing which way she had gone—up: toward where the road ended in the hills after the last empty house; or down: to cars, stores, the bus station.

He stood there, perhaps hoping to see her small figure on the road getting larger, and he remembered the scene on the beach: her girl children moving away from her and back, her laugh he thought he had heard. He stood there, the flakes

15

rushing down the road past him, until one arm and one leg were nearly white and his feet were as void of feeling as the roots of trees beneath the frozen earth. The trucks did not pass or return. Perhaps she had ridden off in one. The air grew white around him, the snow falling thicker and faster, blowing almost horizontally past him, one side of his face already having little more feeling than his feet. He pictured the artist's wife in an overheated bus headed south. At times he could almost see her face in the whirling snow.

Eventually he had no choice but to continue down the road himself. After a few minutes moving at his own pace, he had warmed up. He stopped to brush the snow from his arm and leg and, starting again, the wind at his back and the way tending downhill, he was even enjoying the unseasonable storm driving past him. His last taste of winter, he told himself, as if the purpose of the weather was to fix its impressions upon him, and he found himself thinking of the artist's wife in New York. He imagined her blown around some windy corner at him: she is moving rapidly, brightly, a large canvas under her arm. She sees him. There is the moment of recognition, her lips opening . . . But no, of course; he realizes it is impossible: she doesn't know him, he doesn't know her. They pass each other without a word.

As if in a final, triumphant fling, the storm settled down in earnest around him. At a division in the road he even chose the wrong way, perhaps unconsciously attempting to keep the storm at his back. This road narrowed and dropped away suddenly and, becoming aware of the unfamiliarity of his surroundings, he stopped and was about to fight his way back up to the right turning, when something to the side caught his eye.

She was sitting very still in a sheltered spot, her back against one of the few large trees. It was the brightness of her coat that he had noticed, even though it was partly concealed by snow. He practically had to wade over to her through the fallen branches. Again she was facing somewhat away from him. Standing at her side, he touched her shoulder. He removed his gloves and placed the backs of his fingers gently against her cheek. He took her face in both hands. Then, slipping them behind her neck, underneath her soft hair, he put his own face against hers, moving it lightly over her eyes, her mouth, speaking her name just loudly enough for her to hear. But her head did not move, her eyes did not open. Putting his arms around her he tried to lift her, but the stiffness in her body resisted him.

He stood looking at her. She looked just like a child sitting in the snow. And he . . . ? He was an older man. Around them, between them, the gray flakes fell.

The Shadow of the Mountain

He was already exhausted. The second trail up the mountain rose more steadily, if less quickly, than the first. The reins hanging unneeded over the horn, the horse was a moving platform of warm flesh and bone that followed the horse in front of him, the guide's horse, and the guide's horse went where he was aimed. He himself was a man's burden of hope and fear and memory.

What was she wearing? How did she wear her hair now? Was she twenty still, looking at him with full eyes? Love, she said, was the search of the human soul for completion. Sometimes the search was successful, sometimes not. To penetrate to the essential nature of the loved one is to understand life itself. Her words. Her essay, read to him on a wildly tossing airplane twenty years ago. He heard again her intonation, her voice. Love changes, she said, and she was right. He remembered the warmth next to his in the dark and he saw himself bringing that up, as positive identification, through a translator or in his own broken words, to some dark little chief of police, saw the man's teeth slowly becoming visible.

The first time they had been going to take their youth (or hers) to Tahiti. The idea came to them on the elevated train creaking high above the shadows of the city. Or it came to them holding hands on the corner of Randolph and State, in front of Marshall Field's, braving the wintry blast. Or it came to them

18

in a little restaurant off Michigan Avenue called Le Petit Gourmet. It came with the aperitif and they talked of nothing else until the liqueur. He had hesitated, then decided. He made provision for his first wife, his children, and strode off with a suitcase listening to his heart.

Giggling in the passport office, kissing in taxis, that existence already a panorama shrinking behind them, like kids they dropped everything, sold everything and bought their tickets. Then the war interfered. Suddenly the French cancelled their visas and they were left standing with their suitcases.

"*Going* is somehow part of it, isn't it?" he had asked.

"Of course," she had said.

And they went to Mexico where they didn't have to worry about U-boats or Vichy French or whatever.

The mad DC3 dropping into air pockets over the Sierra Madre, in Chihuahua, already nervous, they learned what *cerveza* was. In Torreón, terrified, they got off to continue their journey by train. In Cuernavaca they rented a house. It was cheap then. In a time of disturbance, cautioned by their good Mexican neighbors that *gringoes* weren't safe on the streets, they barricaded themselves in the solid old sixty-dollar house and survived. After that he carried a .38 in his coat pocket. The one time the taxi driver and his brother took off with them down a dark street he didn't have it, but reaching into the pocket where he usually carried it and saying *hombre* in his deepest warning guttural was just as good.

They had a child. The child had dysentery for a year and a day. Left alone for the briefest period, he would be covered with excrement when they returned. He didn't understand why he couldn't eat, never did understand. And the man remembered his healthy children in Chicago and wondered. But the child was beautiful, exceptionally intelligent—and

19

easily dissatisfied. Some days he looked like him, other days he looked like her. He had a wonderful, deeply amused laugh you could hear in the garden, and waved his tiny arms and legs in time with any music. On the second Christmas the child died. It was buried in the hard yellow soil, in hallowed ground. The coffin was so tiny he carried it in his arms. They took it out in a taxi. The taxi waited, having agreed beforehand on the price.

Then they were just the two of them again. For a while they grew pale and lost weight. A certain amount of their substance seemed to follow the child. Then, slowly, their color returned, their energies revived. He decided he was still young. There was still time for this second life, possibly even a third. He began to study ruins, ancient gods, dead peoples. She began to keep a journal, events of her day, tiny sketches, watercolors. Then she was pregnant again, sitting in the garden, the long warm days of the Cuernavaca summer, full, waiting, feeding her child-to-be on poetry, folk tales, history, reading to him silently. Then it was her turn for dysentery. She lost the child one night. After that she was better, and said she understood their life was for just the two of them. And one afternoon, a week or two later, he heard a shot and ran upstairs to find her standing dazed in the center of the room, the .38 still smoking in her hand.

After that, they sat in the garden again. There was a new crispness in the autumn nights. And a new silence. And the absurd feeling of something missing, a feeling unknown to their first passionate acquaintance. In the middle of the third year, they suddenly left. The crazy airplane ride, the *cerveza* well known by now, along with stronger stuff, the dizzy views of the Sierra Madre, and then El Paso, Texas, gas stations and ice cream, the dumb, dumb faces, the end of the war.

Twenty years later they were back, quieter, claiming less for themselves, ageing (she too). They had lasted anyway. His children now seemed as old as she. They had had a child who lived, conceived and raised in the big city, but they didn't understand him, he didn't understand them. Retracing the path of their first happiness, somewhat awash in the memory of that poetic time, their daring runaway youth (his too, though it had only arrived in his forties), they didn't mind the dream-like woosh of the jet. They had left the driving years behind them when they circled out of O'Hare, the cold hard lights of Chicago dipping under the wing.

The sixty-dollar house was gone. A highway had ploughed right through it. Mexico was a land gone mad with engineers. They went further, stumbling down the ramp in Oaxaca and Tuxtla Gutierrez before the backfiring taxi wound away with them into the mountains, in the general direction of the Guatemalan border. The unfamiliar mountain Indians with their hard dark legs and beribboned hats seemed distant and picturesque. And they had a hazy impression of a stupid altercation at the ranch when, in spite of the universal respect for cash and prepaid reservations, they had nearly been turned away when they had to be led from the car for a long sleep before they could appreciate the violent rain, the flat-eyed men standing silent under the eaves, the horses waiting patiently under the trees.

At dinner the first night they sat across from each other, almost glad to be out of Mexico in a way, for the ranch was American-owned and Mexico was no longer Mexico. They ate their fill, not talking to the other guests, sure of their own image, not really interested in it anymore. Yet, looking through the cigarette smoke at each other, he saw a woman who had not arrived with him, who was still wandering behind her eyes, and she saw a man who was not the man who had carried her south twenty years ago.

And, after a while, they knew they had not spoken to each

21

other either and they looked away, at nothing, at the antiqued furniture (the image of the ranch), the dark Mexican night outside the window, then back again.

"Well?" he said.

She did not respond.

"Well, what do you feel?" he asked.

"Nothing," she answered immediately.

"You're here, aren't you?" He was aware of the warmth in his own voice, and the impatience.

"I don't know," she answered after a moment, and attempted a smile.

A large stone kicked loose by her horse clattered down the steep, flood-eroded trail, before sailing into the air, clearly missing the dark head of the guide. She heard it clattering again far below as he stopped, turning around in his saddle to look back up at her. Eyes that understood good luck and bad, she thought, cruelty, the joy of escape. Was he smiling? His horse, standing still, exhaled loudly. The sweat ran down its sides in long dark streaks. Facing forward again, the guide sat motionless, doing nothing. She stretched one sore leg, then the other. Her horse would move when his did. The valley, capped overhead in mist, lay open below. She could see the dark gash in its middle, the rocky hole the soil-colored water disappeared into after each sudden drenching, the water pouring into and off the mountain, leaving a different track for the horse to follow that day and the next.

They were moving again. It seemed straight down. She leaned back in the saddle trying to let her feet in the stirrups take her shifting weight as the somewhat rested horse picked its way towards the valley. That afternoon the guide had led her further than ever across the mountain. The Indian women, sitting in clearings with their goats and their children, had

22

disappeared into the trees at their approach. Like the water, she thought, pouring down the mountain almost every afternoon, leaving nothing, not a pool, not a cupful for drinking. But little patches of corn thrived on oddly-shaped fields thrusting right up into the trees on either side of the trail.

That afternoon in the driving wind-pushed rain they had found partial shelter in the angular overhang of a fallen boulder. Corn grew absurdly all around it. They sat on their horses for warmth, their ponchos pulled over their heads, not looking at one another, the guide silent, immobile, unconcerned. After the rain a young hummingbird had landed on her head, its little feet clinging in her hair until it flew away, whirring, vertical, already graceful, its fire-red throat flashing in the sun. And her heart flew up too, for the first time after such silence, such silent years, as if it had just been waiting, as if she were a child again and had been blessed. Once more the mystery had touched her, perhaps for only the second time in her life, as if she were a young girl still and could speak.

In the brilliant sun after the rain, in the clamor of the insects she couldn't see, and of the birds who saw the insects but left them buzzing she and the guide had sat beside the horses resting, eating and drinking what he carried in his saddlebag. She had looked at all this difference: the close, empty sky, the house-size rocks, the trees. She had thought of the world before man, the sunless earth beneath the forest, the peace of empty places, and then humankind, and then the bird and time passing and herself. She had not looked at him when she spoke. She didn't speak his language. He spoke no other. She had felt him looking at her as a horse does, or a dog waiting for her to finish. And she had told him of her love, the house in Cuernavaca, her dead children, her bad shot with the .38, the bullet hole in the ceiling.

When she did turn towards him, he looked away, usually

up, at nothing, but a nothing that held his eyes unmoving until she stopped looking at him. Eyes hard, unrevealing as stones, then soft, yielding, temporary like the brief pools of brown water before the earth swallowed them up. He would not pretend he understood. He would not be humbled by her unintelligible words. Then he had spoken to her, without anger, words that meant nothing to her arriving on his lips at the same pace, the same volume, one after the other until it was her turn to look away and down and she regretted speaking.

Once, at the door after a day-long ride, he had stood holding both horses in the sudden long rays of light that preceded the dark. She had made him wait, had hurried up the stairs and back, her legs exhausted and trembling, finally tumbling the little cans of evaporated milk into his hands. She had wondered where he lived—she had seen him riding back up the mountain at dusk—if he had a wife or child, if they would know how to open the cans. He had smiled then (she could hardly forget that), leading the horses away with one hand, the little white cans reflecting the sun in the other.

And one night a sound had called her, called to something in her, drawn her outside and she had stood on the cool wet grass in her nightgown listening to the shadowy figures of the horses moving about her in the moonlight and the mist, heard their teeth tearing the grass, had spotted her own horse moving amongst the others and slowly approached, standing at his side while he tore the grass near her bare feet. But when she put her hand out he had moved instantly away, lowering his head to eat again out of her reach, this horse who had carried her day after day, whom she had spoken to in a language she felt sure he understood. Then he was gone and she had seen the guide's horse and the guide, or the shadow of the guide made large by the blanket over his shoulders, the stillness of the

24

night, the rifle in his hand. Then he was gone too. The mist
settled more thickly. The horses were further away, still audible, still eating the fresh wet grass. And whatever called her
out had held her standing until she was shaking with the cold
and she returned to lie like a corpse in her bed, stiff and
motionless until the first light.

The horse, throwing up its head, returned her to the moment. The guide stopped. Her horse stopping of its own ac-
cord nearly at his side, she saw the impassable breach in the
downward plunge of the escarpment, the washed-out trail, and
far beneath the shadow of the mountain, the now-familiar
buildings, the tiny lights winking on already in the kitchen
windows, the darkness in her own where she felt sure her silent
thinking husband stared out at the fading light. Secretly she
had hoped these summer rains would water him, that he would
grow again in these green shadows, his spirit riding out alone
again, the lone figure in that great valley, looking for her. And
she felt like standing up in the stirrups, waving and shouting,
a silly miniscule figure on the rim of the mountain, unheard
and unseen. Then she noticed the flat eyes of the guide, un-
excited, undismayed as he slipped to the ground, turning first
his horse around, then hers, leading her back up the mountain
in the sudden thickening darkness. And without protest, without a sound, she allowed herself to be carried into the night.

Was happiness possible on this earth? Three lives had at least
raised the question. He was not ready for the fourth. When he
had first arrived the head man, open to gifts, gave permission
to wear the Indian costume. A day of that was enough. Better
just to think oneself a fool. Further away than ever, that life
always thriving around a corner, behind a door, he had sat in
the marketplace with tears in his heart. And fear and mortality
and irretrievable time.

25

In the beginning they had all ridden together, a long bumbling line strung out on the side of the mountain, the sun too near, even the bugs protesting, the vegetation screaming at him, glaring. He was too old for this, too pale, his body not conditioned. Should he fall off the ants would whiten his bones before the guide could turn his horse around to see what happened. Once a hummingbird, detaching itself from the sky, had suddenly darted to within five feet of his face, hovering there, looking at him, flashing its brilliant throat like the magic bird of . . . Of what? He thought of Montezuma, beautiful delicate man, under a canopy of green feathers, with golden soles on his shoes and lords to sweep the ground on which he trod.

At dinner a native of the conquering race would continue to lecture him on art, decorative art that masks and brightens the face of arbitrary nature: the floods, the droughts, the terrifying storms from the gulf. He would not mention the empty sky, of course, the empty sky that is worst of all and a wife looking up into it. He would listen and not listen, his mind a terrifying blank on which, if he could not and would never sing hosannas, he should be copying the stone work with a clenched and trembling fist, or inscribing the minute and exacting history of those last days . . .

He thought of teeming markets, a stone calendar turning up centuries later, of fabulous gardens, aviaries, the zoo (a well-fed human albino, strange life from the hot lands to the east), torchlight ceremonies on the temples and priests with blood-drenched stinking hair, the birds, a robe of feathers for a complex aristocratic ruler, the years passing, slowly at first, the courage, the history of a people, the city in the lake, then the years coming faster, tumbling one over the other, the recorded dates, soldiers' journals, the end . . .

And now, where was the life that should be recorded? Once,

in his forties, he had sensed all errors erased, all life before him, a brilliant sensuous woman in his arms . . . He had *run* with their suitcases, *run* through the airport, just in time, the plane already warming up, the blast from the propellors whipping his hair, his suit, her long dress plastered against her body, his breath coming easily and deep. Oh, the strength of it! And now?

The rains always followed the sun, drowning the live chatter in the undergrowth, substituting their own steady drone. It had rained on him at the end of the line of dull uninterested horses. It rained on the red tiles now over his head, dampening the atmosphere still further, oppressing the valley beyond his window, the low roofs of the village in the distance, not a single human figure in sight though he could see miles, miles. Alone in one more temporary room, looking out past damp plaster walls, the rotting wooden frame of the window, he thought only: afternoon rain, the middle years, a wife riding on the mountain. His biological clock told him, among other things, that the time for her return had passed. He began to pace the room, slowly at first, then faster, burdened with the absurd illogical feeling that all had been lost in the last ten minutes. He tried to picture her, saw her riding naked in the rain, her legs around a steaming horse, and he was afraid.

It began to rain, the simple straight-down night rain, without wind, without sound, soaking everything, penetrating her poncho around her neck, soaking first her collar then her back, entering over the tops of her boots where there was a gap beneath the heavy rubber flaps, the damp rising on the sides of her legs and running down her ankles until she heard her toes squishing in her boots. The trail was levelling off. Sitting straighter in the saddle, shifting the pain in her legs, she felt the dark presence of the trees muffling the rain and watched the long rope with which the guide led her disappearing into the darkness in front of her. Still alert enough to hope that either he or his horse could see in the dark, tales of other nights told before the fireplace wandered in her mind: of the artist who had drawn the women on the mountain when the men were away, and of the men coming home and finding their women's souls already possessed in his sketchbook, of the artist being packed out again without his head and the *Federales* riding in to subdue the mountain and riding out again at one-third strength, the mountain still wild and ancient and unsubdued.

Almost asleep, the cessation of sound woke her, the clatter of the trail gone, her horse walking on a bed of pine needles when an unseen branch slapped her across the face. A little later when he stopped, she did not move, still holding the side of her face, grateful for the end of motion, for the horse's heat rising under her poncho. Left in the saddle she felt her horse tied up by the other and the guide moving about her, invisible, almost soundless, until she heard the dry wood being dragged close, cracking and breaking, until she saw a spark and his cupped hands and a small still flame growing slowly larger, beginning to flicker and snap at the pine needles, the carefully added twigs and smaller branches.

A rock wall thrust up abruptly overhead, rising and falling with the fire, gray, cold looking—and dry. The interlacing branches of the trees were thick and low, protective, forming almost a pocket in the side of the mountain. The air was drier too, cold and still, the soft rain inaudible beyond the trees, only the breath of dampness drawing into the fire asserting its presence and continuation. She almost started. The guide, his fire made, was standing a little behind her watching her watch the rock wall and the trees. He moved slightly when she saw him, picking up a stone which he threw into a hole, a darker shadow in the rock she had paid no attention to, and listening, encouraging her to listen. She heard the stone click once or twice on its downward plunge, then nothing. He looked at her, apparently waiting. Perhaps he was amused by the hollow bottomless mountain. Perhaps he was amusing her.

He moved towards her suddenly, silently helping her off her horse, usually unnecessary, she usually stood a full head taller than he, lifting and setting her down as if she were weightless, and she crumpled at his feet, her legs unwilling to support her. Lifted and set down again near the fire she had to make an effort to believe or even remember his effortless strength. The magic of the heat penetrating her body lulled her. The steam rising from her legs was amazing, the glow seen through half-closed eyes, the ebb and flow of color in the depth of the wood was miraculous, a movement in her too, and the fire-light, the still dry cup that held her in the side of the mountain, almost a vision.

Somehow managing to lift her head once, she saw the eyes across the fire on her, infinitely patient, almost warm. And seeing her head come up suddenly, her eyes wide open, he smiled for the second time in her memory, almost laughed, then signalled briefly with his hand for her to put her head down again and she did, falling at once into the surprising calm in her, the occasional sound of burning sticks further away and further, then gone.

He watched the night outside the window, thick heavy rain-drops entering the light, rushing straight down, continuous as a cold shower left running, solid, silent beyond the glass, like streaks of water frozen in the air. He looked at the emptiness across from him, unable to displace the feeling of something

29

unsaid still in him, something still waiting to be said. And he kept himself from running out into the rain screaming by the thought that she still *was*, was somewhere, anywhere, even galloping full speed away from him.

Dawn, an enormous flat sun rising right over him, blatant, white hot like savage unworkable metal. The shortcut to the mountain rose steeply overhead. They did not progress. The guide seemed the same guide who had taken his wife into the mountain: silence, a face inexpressive as rock and sparkling eyes. Nothing changed. No matter how high the horses climbed, the black hole in the center of the valley remained black. And the mountain rose straight and green and gray overhead, silent and untelling and alive. And his thoughts were like wind upon it, a wind that would overwhelm no trees.

At the steepest incline, where the uneven climbing of the horse worked the horn into his stomach, the guide stopped suddenly. In front of them the trail was gone, a distance of twenty or thirty feet impassable with or without horses. Above him he could see it disappearing into the first tall dark pines of the mountain. Without a sound the guide passed him riding back down the trail. After a moment staring hopelessly across the gap for himself, he turned his horse without difficulty and followed him.

The sun entered her nest for a moment, falling on the ashes of the night's fire, the stiff dried legs of her pants. Then it was gone. She lay still a moment, looking around her in the half-light, listening to the silence. The insects of the valley did not enter the forest. Pushing aside the dry needles which stuck to her skin, standing painfully, brushing her hands slowly one against the other, she felt the soreness of one hip, one arm, the whole side of her body she had slept on motionlessly to save her warmth. Uncertain and without strength she stepped out from under the thick branches.

The horses were gone. The guide was gone. She found a warm rock outside her nest and lowered herself onto it to wait for his return. An hour later she was hungry, a hunger unknown to her body. Fingering the few dried-out berries in the clearing, she didn't dare put anything in her mouth. Suddenly thirst was worse than hunger. There was no water on the mountain. Water rushed through the soil, the crevices, disappearing into the dark insides of the rock, audible for a day after in the strange gash in the center of the valley before the silence and the birds and then the rains began again.

Of course. The guide had led the horses to the water. It was proverbial. They would return with full bellies and dripping muzzles. The man would smile holding out the clear cool liquid to her in cupped hands. She would drink like a horse, her head bent low, drawing the water silently through her lips. When the sun was overhead she remembered that the most foolish thing you could do was to leave the one spot where you had last been seen.

By late afternoon it was clear to her the guide was not returning. Thirst led her around the edges of the clearing, looking under the dense branches, feeling with her hands, squeamishly, then desperately. She saw herself finding the way to the valley suddenly, all at once, falling faster than it is possible to fall into the dark hole in its middle, praying that in its depths there would be cool black water. Forcing her way through, tearing her clothes, scratching her face and arms, she found the thick mud already turning gray and hard around the edges. Yet the handfuls she was able to claw out and squeeze in her handkerchief released a few drops of dark water into her mouth.

Thirst relaxing its total domination of her mind, she be-

31

came aware of herself with hands and face she could not clean, crouching half-tangled in the roots and branches of a bush that had already scratched her several times. Like a child, she thought, forgotten at its play, unfed, with sticky hair. Until this moment she had always been the one witholding her presence, the one who needed to be alone. Once again solitude had happened to her, as it had happened only once or twice before in her life, and she was a young woman again with her children gone and out of reach, or a child herself, and without reason it seemed she began to cry, falling over helplessly against the bush as the pain of feeling surged again and again through her body.

And she found herself screaming absurdly, yelling her location to the mountain, to anyone, anything, the guide, a bird, then catching her breath as the silence rushed back at her and even the air in her lungs became still. Suddenly she wanted to leap up and run and just as suddenly, still half-tangled in the bush, she slipped to the ground and her eyes closed and the sun beat down on her head.

In her mind it was night, and she thought of the night and fire, of the three sacred stones of the hearth, of the god of fire and the god of the night sky who saw in a mirror of obsidian all the events of the world. And she saw herself, then and now, the life given up too soon, too easily, the long living death and a dream of wild youth and dead children, her own far-away eyes, her non-answers and unknown invisible love, the death spreading out from her like silence. And now, too late, the anger and the hate overflowing, her dry teeth grinding, scratching in her skull, her fists like rocks upon the ground, she pressed her face into the mud and lay still.

The horse had come to a stop. There was a fork in the trail. The guide had already dismounted. Taking a stick he scratched in the faded powdery soil. The fork was the lower end of a giant loop, the two ends of which came together further on. There was no telling which branch his wife would be descending. Now he would take one and the guide would take the other. Whoever arrived first where the trails rejoined would simply wait. At least that was how he understood it. But if he found his wife he was to return with her. The guide would know from the hoof marks what had happened, and he pointed at the earth, smiling.

An hour later the horse became unmanageable. Kicking it, slapping it across the head with the end of the reins had no effect. It only wanted to turn and gallop down the mountain. Perhaps he had missed the coming together of the trail. The shadows were lengthening, the horse's hooves rang in the silence. The insects were gone. There were no birds. There were no more little patches of corn, only the great rocks the trail wound among, this way, then that. Perhaps he had ridden into a dead spot on the mountain where, due to some peculiarity of light or air, nothing lived or moved or breathed, except himself and the horse—and the mountain, which brooded here, or silently despaired, or was depressed and without feeling. Then the horse rose and threw him and was gone.

He had landed on his face, it seemed, mostly on his chin, but blood was dripping from his nose and when he moved to touch it he found his forearm turned at an unnatural angle from his elbow. Sitting up in the middle of the trail, finding himself completely covered with its white dust, he had an almost overwhelming urge to stumble up and run back down the trail after the horse. Trembling all over, chilled with his own sweat and clenching his teeth against the noise they made, he looked painfully around him. Only the great rocks remained looming over him, huge and irregular, outlined against the coming dark, and the blood drops falling regularly from his nose seemed almost black on his white dusted legs.

Somehow, slowly, the silence entered him, and he sat very still, far from words, for once not even trying to think and just then noticing

33

Venus in the west and another star or planet close below it. Removing his shirt with difficulty, he fastened the broken arm as well as he could to his waist, tying a knot with the other hand and his teeth. A few paces further he came upon the upper junction of the trail. The guide had not been there. His wife had not descended the other way. There were no prints of any kind.

Waiting, he knew, for nothing, standing still in the deepening shadows beneath the trees, he found himself wondering about the justice of the Indians, or whatever it was, and wondering what he was doing on the side of the mountain in the fading light and then the darkness. And he felt he heard her voice then, heard it distinctly, her own hesitant response, not terrified, perhaps not even afraid, just reminding, claiming his attention as only a whisper could, and the first heavy drops of rain were startling.

Moonlight still revealed the trail in the exposed places. He more or less picked his way under the trees. Discovering a sense of direction he didn't know he had, he felt the ranch distinctly at his back, somewhat below him, and the unknown, the mountain, growing larger as he approached, the night clouds gathering about its head, adding to its bulk, the mountain larger than the sky.

When she opened her eyes the east side of the mountain was in shadow and the sky overhead was a colorless void caught between night and day. Just before dark she crawled back into her nest, finding hurriedly with her fingers the few remaining twigs and tiny branches from the little pile the guide had used to build the fire. Her work gradually becoming visible, she twirled one small stick between her palms, drilling it Indian-fashion into a larger piece of wood upon the ground. The energy finally leaving her exhausted hands, it seemed at that moment to enter and glow in a few minute slivers torn off with her nails and set against the point of contact of the spinning stick. Her hands numb senseless things on the ends of her arms, blowing softly with pursed lips, she persisted until the first tiny flame seemed to appear from nowhere.

Later, standing still in the clearing, her fire behind her, she noticed the movement of the stars against the overhanging blackness of the branches and saw the night clouds forming above the rim and rising higher, adding to the shadow of the mountain. She was nothing herself at that moment, perhaps a waiting, a response. But there was no longer any citadel to guard, no golden past to preserve. Only this moment, perhaps best of all, and the mountain rising straight up, claiming, extinguishing the sky. In the first heavy drops she began to clean her hands, then her face. And in the last light from the stars the few berries glistened on the bush, as if they only revealed themselves at night or only then lost the dusty inedible look of day, swelling up with the water that fell from the sky. Snatching several, she hurried into her nest as the dripping suddenly became a flood, beating on the earth of the mountain, washing what it could of it away.

She set a piece of bark outside to catch the rain, reaching out for it several times, feeling the cold certain drops on her wrist and tasting a cool clear liquid she did not remember ever drinking before. She kept her fire small and steady, conserving her coals and wood, conserving also the unexpected feeling of being at home, of waiting for someone to come home to her.

Walls

The sun did not seem to be more than a couple of hundred yards off the surface of the earth. The air moved meaninglessly through the few trees. The moving leaves had lost all color to the dust, and were now hardly more than moving aspects of the colorless hills or the colorless sky. They were the same temperature too. After allowing a few swallows of water from one of the bottles in the back of the Rover to run down his throat, Jeff had dropped down near the edge of the dark hole of the well. He exhaled slowly and extended his fingers, still aching from the violent twistings of the wheel. Every motion of his body was an effort now; he regretted that he could not just step out of that overheated vehicle too. He smeared protective lotion on his forehead and nose, on his neck and arms, and on his lips. He blew the dust off his sunglasses and looked around him.

Nothing. The hills like dumped piles of gravel, hopeless piles of sand. The wrong end of the hourglass, he thought, days of his life running out of him beneath an empty sky. He tried to imagine dark, swelling clouds overhead, a few cool drops falling on his face, but it was not possible. And in the emptiness he noticed two faraway hawks soaring nearer, circling, invisibly connected, one to the other. He raised his binoculars, finding them again. Leaning backwards, he followed their movements, still trying to imagine: the air in solid motion, possibly cool . . .

Training his binoculars on the infinite waste below, Jeff swept the middle distance; within that well-defined circle sliding across sand and rock, even the unlimited seemed bearable; his fellow travelers moved beneath the sun like tired, lost ants: Eric and Erica, man and wife, unspeaking, drifting about each other at different speeds—her legs slow and weak, patches of sweat visible on her inappropriate tight pants; his all thin, nervous muscle extending from his shorts, his camera sparkling beneath his neck like a shining talisman. He seemed to be looking for something that could only be found at a great distance—if at all. Again the circle slid across the waste, and the binoculars seemed to burn in his hands and burn against his eyes. His wife: and he knew her stance, her clothing, even before he recognized her consciously, her thin hair and strained features; now Anna crouched, holding something close to her face, then stood, looking around her, and her eyes seemed to meet his in the dark tunnel of the lens. Now Thomas, colleague, appeared silently behind her; together they spoke the distant, inaudible words and wandered off, looking at the ground.

Behind them a breath of wind picked up the loose dust, whirling it a hundred yards along the surface before it settled. Then the wind was invisible; then it was flowing through the dust-colored leaves above him, though he felt nothing, nothing, and the air around him remained motionless and uncooled, and painful to the hand moving through it. He lowered the binoculars. The figures were gone—Eric and Erica, Anna, Thomas, out of sight in some depression. The hawks were gone. The waste remained, pure and indifferent, as if it had never been encroached upon, as if it could never matter in the least who came and went upon it. He replaced his sunglasses. He threw a stone in the well. A moment's delay, and then a final, distant click, rock on rock. He glanced up at the trees, now motionless again. Then the silence entered him too, and he closed his eyes. "Ring loud," he repeated to himself; and he felt he was still wrestling with the vibrations, with the sudden, unanticipated veerings of the vehicle: "Ring loud," "Ring loud with the grief and delight," "Ring loud . . ."

"Are you asleep?" she asked.

Something mixed in him with weakness leaving a faint nausea. What was it? The weight of the burning air on him had been like . . . like what? Was the body confused? He opened his eyes. Erica—her hair suffused with light, her skin dusted with innumerable grains of sand; Erica stood at the back of the Land-Rover, carelessly helping herself to the water. She seemed unaware of the rivulets running down her chin. Her breath was coming fast and he could see the veins in her neck, and her own wetness: under her arms, her breasts, and up the crack of her behind. Her slow movements halted at last, she seemed to be drying up under her eyes, her entire body lightening in color.

Erica felt her sides, which had been dripping a moment ago, already uncomfortably dry and burning. She raised her hand to her armpit, also already dry, and wondered how long it would take her to dry up completely. And she looked at Jeff, sitting dazed on the other side of the well, his head at an angle, his dark, deep-set eyes half closed—as if a big hand had come down out of the sky and grazed him, leaving him momentarily stunned, an easy target for the second swat. She ran her fingers through her hair, and her hand made a sound like a small animal scurrying through dry grass. Then she wiped her lips, though her lips were dry before the back of her hand had reached them.

"Why aren't you looking?" she asked. The words seemed unwilling to leave her throat, and the last ones had to be pushed with what force remained in her upper chest.

He smiled self-consciously, but didn't answer, and almost unnoticed, the silence returned. After a moment, she too threw a stone in the well.

"Nothing," she said.

"Nothing," he said.

"Rest," she said, placing her hand briefly on his forehead as she passed. She settled herself in the faint shade and closed her eyes. She felt the sand to either side of her, her hands moving in large, slow circles. She felt the air moving in and out of her lungs, and the slow beating of her heart. That was it: this land was under water, really. It was all an underwater scene. She remembered the damp sand she had thrust her hand into, just beneath the smooth, dry surface of a dune. Under water the sun was not so unfriendly. Now she lifted and let fall a handful of sand. Soft, tingley sand, now dry, dry again, dry like the discarded heart and the tongues of lizards. As a child she had let the sand run through her fingers. Now, if she wanted to, she could dribble the fine grains on her full breasts or fill the smooth, dry depression of her navel. Days, weeks, years. She imagined her body still changing, evolving, beneath the burning revolutions of the sun, beneath the patter of a single handful of sand. Into what? For a moment there were tears in her eyes. Then she wondered where the tears had gone.

Restless, she stood up suddenly and approached the edge of the deep, unwalled well to a spot where she might see to the very bottom without falling in. But she could not see anything. In a dry sea of blinding light, impenetrable darkness, nothing. And the desert was nothing, she thought. Why should she care what lived or breathed or moved upon it? She looked up. The sky was nothing too. And she? What was she?

Desolation of the . . . Of the what, she wondered. And what is there to do if nothing moves upon that surface?

"Why aren't you?" he asked.

"What?" She nearly jumped, but maintained her footing on the edge.

"Why aren't you looking?"

She turned on him. "Because there is nothing to be found, is there? Do you believe there is anything to be found?"

He shrugged.

"If there is, you won't be the one to find it." She stopped herself, wondering at the sound of her own voice.

"Who will?" he asked quietly.

She looked at Jeff, his half bitter, half ironical eyes, the half smile that almost, but not quite, lifted the corners of his mouth; and she thought of big, friendly Thomas; and of her intense, silent husband with his faraway look, and the camera in which he would entrap all life if he could, capturing past, present and future with a single soft and perfect click. And she thought of herself and of Anna: memory and depression, inner workings and not enough time, not half enough time . . .

"I don't think any of us were ever meant to find anything," she said.

"Look at him through the binoculars," said Anna, focusing the glasses and handing them to Erica.

Another well. A lush growth of date palms, unharvested, abandoned, the untouched and wasted fruit presiding over shadowed silence, and over a deep pool of water, the weeds swaying long and cool and green on the bottom. On the stone rim two red dragonflies paused, their eyes mobile, their parked wings sparkling gold and silver in the mottled light.

"Look into his eyes and read his thoughts," said Anna.

"I can't see anything," said Erica, swaying strangely as she looked through the glasses, unable to find the stationary drag-onfly.

"To the left," said Anna, watching her.

"Oh, yes."

"That's the other one."

"Is it?"

"What's she thinking?" asked Anna.

"She?" Erica lowered the glasses. "The same thing, of course." And she smiled at Anna, who smiled at the same time. "But are you sure it's a she?"

Erica carefully handed back the glasses. For a moment they were both holding onto them.

"Haven't you noticed how everything comes in pairs in the desert?" asked Anna. "Is it so difficult to find a member of the same species?" she laughed. "Or is it just that, given the absence of undergrowth and natural cover, it is easier for us to observe . . ."

"Perhaps they are afraid," suggested Erica quietly.

"Of what?" asked Anna.

They entered a mud dwelling on a slight rise, consisting of one small, empty room, pristine as if recently swept. One arched window, never intended to hold glass, faced into the shadow of the trees. A small, ceiling high alcove seemed at first to be a well-swept fireplace. But there were no signs of a fire and no outlet for the smoke. An accumulation of neatly folded material in a corner proved to be once bright, sheer and clinging dresses, such as the native women wore beneath their all-concealing black veils. Anna picked one up between her fingertips, holding it at arm's length.

"Shall we put them on and wait for the men?" she suggested.

Erica just touched the flimsy, seductive material of another, holding it up until she could see the light through it.

41

MICHAEL McGUIRE

"Let's," she smiled suddenly, her childish laughter rising from some forgotten depths. Together, they hurriedly removed their blouses and undid their belts. Their pants half down (one knee ready to come up), their eyes met. Stooped, half naked, white, suddenly almost heavy and awkward, their lower legs constrained, they faced each other.

"No, I don't think so; do you?" smiled Anna. Her voice was dry, rhetorical.

"Not really," agreed Erica, straightening, pulling up her pants.

Together they replaced their blouses and stood still a moment, not doing anything. Beyond the arched window the date palms swayed like seaweed in a steady, softly audible wind. In the semidarkness the soft material of the discarded dresses fluttered lightly on the floor. When they stepped out underneath the sun again, the unframed immensity almost drove them back, and the burning air entered them, reaching deeper than before. Shielding their eyes, they saw beyond the tiny, walled plantation; beyond their own miniscule tracks curving out from the dry riverbed, leading directly to the Land-Rovers parked under the first palms. Stopped again by an awareness of the surrounding silence, as if nature had paused just long enough for something to leap upon them, and the recurrence of her small sounds would be sufficient to mark their passing, both stared at the blank, surrounding hills, and at the wadi, widening into nothing.

Brainlike, the small, rough, pinkish rock with its wormy surface lay neatly cracked in two beneath a cloudless sky. The two halves still facing each other directly, the split might have occurred last night or last week, or a thousand years ago. Anna wondered at its interior of sparkling white crystal. She picked up one half, then the other, placing the two together. A

42

perfect fit, she thought, and glancing around her from her squatting position, she was almost surprised to find that there was nothing in particular to look at. Then she opened the stone in her hands and was surprised by its sudden beauty. She wished she knew how it had been formed, how the entire landscape with its senseless litter of small stones had come to be.

She put the two halves in her pocket and stood up. Looking around her again, she saw nothing, for she was more fragile than she thought, or the sun was closer to the earth or heavier in the sky. She was dizzy a moment and raised her hand to her eyes until the feeling passed. Peeking out between her fingers, it seemed she was seeing, for the first time in her life, the natural world: low, gravelly hills, free from almost any form of vegetation; twisting, small dry riverbeds, cutting this way, then that, deepening finally into the wadi. A landscape formed entirely, she thought, by the sudden, brief onslaught of water. Then the water was gone, and the sculpted land remained as the water had left it. For a year, for years, for centuries.

And she . . . ? She would not remain so long. And what great experience had shaped her? And when? She stood still, trying to remember. Looking into the sun, the land was black and invisible against the glare. And when she lowered her hand, she seemed to be standing in the middle of a tideless estuary that had lost even the memory of water. Somehow, she knew, she had stepped out into geologic time and, for a second, she was aware of her own fragile skeleton beneath her skin. Then, in the distance, in the corner of her eye, the binoculars flashed, and she knew she was being watched.

"What is it about this place?"

Thomas appeared behind her and she jumped.

"What . . . I don't know," she said, stepping back from him.

43

"Is it the perspective, the scale of it all?" he went on. "I can't decide whether I want to make love or kill myself." His eyes twinkled and his shaggy, graying beard, sparkling with perspiration, seemed to flow and radiate around his face. "Where is everyone?"

"Alone. Wandering. Collapsed. I don't know," she said. "Jeff is watching us through the binoculars."

Thomas laughed. "Let him watch." They took a few steps in no particular direction. "I was alone and wandering too," he said. They continued a while in silence. "Abraham, Isaac," he spoke again; "it's a story of survival, you know: famine, drought, and grim, desperate reproduction." They walked on, consciously going nowhere. "Sometimes I feel as if I were three inches high," he said, his head slightly bowed, as if it would be too painful to glance around him even once more.

"Have you found anything?" she asked gently.

"Found anything!" said Thomas, recovering himself. "Oh, I'm just pretending to look. I'll make something up when I'm back in the air conditioning. What could I say about this . . . this . . . ? They say when God came upon this He threw up His hands and said: 'Well, boys; what can we do with this?' The boys had no suggestions and God went on to other things."

"And?" asked Anna.

"And?" echoed Thomas.

"Isn't there more to your story?"

"There may be. Odd though, isn't it?"

"What?" she asked.

"That here is where they claim to find Him." And he spread his big arms to encompass the immeasurable, featureless waste.

The surface was crusted and Anna could feel her feet just barely penetrating the crust. She was aware of the footprints she was leaving, not very large, and possibly aimless. But she was more aware of the movement around her. Small, sand-colored grasshoppers hopped, apparently without reason, possibly looking for grass. Larger ones with green, leathery skin and yellow markings waited until approached before leaping away. A shiny black long-legged beetle marched steadily in this direction, then steadily in that. She wondered at a large-eyed lizard who wondered equally at her.

"You see, he likes to be talked to," she said.

"He must be a student of languages," Thomas suggested. "You can be sure he wouldn't cling there listening to one of *them*," he added quietly, wondering why he had never realized in his youth that stones were for throwing, and only that.

"Here you are," said Anna, crouching slowly, her body light and her gesture respecting of distances, her voice gentle, almost caressing. "Here is a bite of something you never bit before."

Thomas crouched slowly behind her, his great head and beard resting childlike on her shoulder. She set a small segment of food inches from the lizard's face, and the lizard never moved, though he was obviously more interested in her than in the food, and only wondered what she was, his thoughts showing themselves clearly in his large, dark eyes.

"Begone!" shouted Thomas suddenly, and the lizard ran fifty feet at breakneck speed and disappeared.

Still crouching before the empty rock, Anna looked over her shoulder at him.

"Why did you do that?" she asked.

"I don't know," he said, and his eyes were wide and innocent as a boy's.

Suddenly Anna was conscious of the wavering air rising from the surface. She felt it pressing against her face like the palm of a big hand pushing her steadily away, and she staggered a little when she stood up.

"Are you all right?" Thomas caught her and held her just as she would have fallen. Her frail body felt like a blade of windblown grass in his great arms, and his hands did not even seem to know they enclosed her small breasts. Suddenly the sky seemed black, and the sun seemed to be beating in her temples and in her chest, a great red sun. Or was it black too? And her breath came in short spurts like water from a pump. But in a moment the sensations had passed and she was able to take her own weight.

"Just leave me here a while," Anna said.

"Are you sure . . ." Thomas began.

"Just leave me," she said.

Thomas released her and turned away. Almost immediately, it seemed to her, he disappeared. She stood still a moment, collecting herself. And for some reason, she remembered that once, many years before, the little birds had landed on her hand to take the seed. What cold, tiny feet, and sharp nails! And how light they had been. How light! Overhead the wet, naked branches had seemed to scratch at the sky, reminding her of the fact that she was not very large either, and she had shivered then, and the birds had flown away . . .

Eric was whittling some stiff, ancient god out of the dry wood. His hands moved quickly, but he did not ruin his god or cut himself. The flying shavings, landing near the fire, curled and darkened on the sand. Why had they come? Why were they here? In his mind he still seemed to be trekking from one dry well to another, the horrible sun setting in his eyes. Whatever they had entered and continued to penetrate, whatever drew them, had transformed itself in infinite, barely perceptible gradations. They had continued on foot up the wadi, discovering another falling away of the land formed by the absent, rushing waters, and still another dry well. Only from this one

46

two pigeons had flown out strongly at their approach. And thirty feet down a log had traversed the shadows, with a few gathered twigs and two eggs resting precariously on one end. Standing on the earth which had once been piled high around the well's edge, it had just been possible with the binoculars to see the end of the wadi.

But, instead of a lake or a depression to explain the flow of water which had shaped the land, only soft, flowing sand was visible, filling the upper end to the very hilltops. And he had speculated on this sand, on how few years or many centuries it had been there, and on the desertion of the wadi, on what must have happened, and on what it might be like now, passing one's life in the silence, in the paralysis of midday, and in the cold, clear desert night. He remembered how the sun had seemed to sink into the sand-stuffed end of the wadi, horribly dry, glaring until the last minute on a land nearly emptied of life. The shadows around them had lengthened dramatically. Every cut in the eroded land, every outcropping, every broken rock had seemed shaped for that moment before sunset when the desert was itself and time was visible, even when there was no one there to see it. At dusk the pigeons had flown back into the well. The wind had risen a little, then dropped away completely. The few dust-covered trees hung motionless over the dark hole in the earth. First Venus had been visible, then Jupiter, and finally the stars, rising one after the other from the bottom of the wadi, while others disappeared as quickly, following Venus over the western edge.

From the beginning it had seemed hopeless to him. What could they hope to find in an arbitrary circle traced on a map? It might as well have been scratched in the sand with a stick. It would have made more sense to "create" a discovery with the camera, or stay at home sipping cool drinks, surrounded by desert landscapes: stunning contrasts in black and white—

dunes curving softly like a woman's thigh. Proceeding at three miles an hour up the dry riverbed, the metal of the lurching vehicle had been untouchable, and turning constantly, there had been no way to avoid the burning sections of the wheel. Sweat had dropped steadily from the end of his nose, and he had wondered why the flesh of his hands did not blister, burn black and smell. Following the first Land Rover, his had been enveloped in a cloud of whitish, powdery dust and when, dead slowly, the oversize tires had climbed the rounded boulders, only to drop savagely on the other side, the dust-laden fumes of his own vehicle had constantly caught up, drifting in the open windows on the still, burning air.

At the first rest he had run his hand over his forehead to find it already dry and resisting friction. And when he had looked at his palm, he had seen the tiny grains of sand lodged in the cracks and pores of his skin. Suddenly, he had been aware of the sand everywhere on his body—on the still damp skin behind his belt, around his ankles inside his socks, and inside his collar, and in his ears and in the cracks around his eyes. And he had wondered how long the five of them could sit there before the sand would bury them, and he had stood up suddenly, shaking his clothes. To the others he had spoken about nothing; he had spoken too loudly and too quickly, and when he had finished, the silence had returned too soon. It was then he had realized that for no good reason he was afraid.

Now all had grown quiet, except for the hard, recurring ticks of the knife on the bit of wood in his hand. Perhaps when he was finished he would stand his god on one of the surrounding hills to survey the scene and pass judgment, or tell him why he was afraid. He had stood there himself today, on hill after hill, the beads of sweat forming on his temples, turning himself slowly, convinced there would be no discovery, seeing nothing in one direction after another. Several times he had begun to remove his camera from its case, but how does one photograph three hundred sixty degrees of horizon and an empty sky? His carving nearly complete, he used the point of his knife to hollow the big, empty eyes, and glanced around him.

Fatigued, dazed, Anna lay on her stomach, looking into the secret heart of the fire. Thomas rested his great head on the backs of her legs, behind her knees, looking at the stars. Erica had closed her eyes, apparently uncertain what or whom to resist. Jeff sat beside her on the sand, watching the few insects march or fly into the flames.

" 'Ring loud with the grief and delight.' "

Jeff was reciting. Erica listened.

" 'Ring loud with grief and delight
Of her dim-silked, dark-haired Musicians
In the brooding silence of night.' "

"What's that?" she asked, not smiling.

" 'Arabia,' " he said, still staring into the fire.

"Who wrote it?"

"Who knows? I can never remember names. Why should we have names? So that it can be said that so-and-so lived so many years and begat so-and-so?"

"Perhaps they come in handy for headstones," she said coolly.

"I prefer *their* cemeteries," he said: "a walled forest of sharp, upright, unnamed stones stuck in the sand. That's more in keeping with our inevitable disappearance, more in keeping with the truth, don't you think?"

"What truth?" Erica asked.

"That we have no names, that it's all lies: Blank, put away your toys; Blank, I love you; Blank, you're dying; that nothing lasts and nothing matters; that we might as well burn our

49

backsides copulating under the murderous sun. Alone we don't need names, of course. But perhaps you think it ought to be Eric talking to Erica, and Anna listening to Jeff? And the Lord said: I will make thy seed as the dust of the earth, as the stars of the heavens; so many shall there be . . ."

Jeff had made his voice particularly deep and godlike, and in spite of herself, Erica giggled.

"Animals don't have names," said Jeff quietly, looking at her.

Her lips coarsened and cracked by the sun, a small drop of blood appeared on the fullest part of her mouth as she faced him.

"What would we have whispered to each other if we had no names?" she asked, smiling and licking it away.

Thomas and Anna moved closer in the cooling night. Sitting close by Jeff and Erica, they formed a primitive circle around the fire. Slowly their bodies realized that they had been let out from under the sun, and that throats cooled with liquid remained damp for more than a few seconds. Bellies full, the desert pushed back by the light, their voices rose with their spirits, offering at last "Old Abdullah Had a Farm" to the magnificence of the night. But such feelings quickly passed. A little later no one spoke, no one slept; the silence and the darkness above the pale, colorless sand seemed to enclose them together, and to come between them as well.

"Sometimes I think I would like to just walk out into the desert," said Eric quietly.

But no one answered him or no one heard, and he was left alone in his awareness of the surrounding darkness, of the vast and peaceful stillness waiting just beyond the ring of silent figures. Later he threw his ancient god into the fire where it flared up briefly. By its light he saw four still, separate bodies, possibly asleep. Later the fire began to smoke a little before going out, smelling faintly of camel. Later the wind moved in the trees, and a faint shower of dust fell on them all. And suddenly Eric was aware that his fear, for brief but definite and recurring patches of time, was leaving him. Like some nocturnal creature, suddenly, secretly free, he was rejoicing in the absence of day and the presence of night.

Somehow now able to move without making a sound, Eric stood and walked away from the lifeless remains of the fire. At the edge of the encampment he looked briefly back at the others. No one stirred. He went on, striding quickly up the wadi, leaning forward to counteract the effect of the sand sliding back with him at every step. Entering further and further the welcoming night, nevertheless, for some time, he had watched his moving shadow deepening on the sand in front of him. And at the top of the wadi he watched the moon rise, huge and distorted in the east. How clear everything was! On an outcropping to his side the shadow of a gray fox moved and met his eyes, followed by another. There was no fear in him now, and raising his arms to better feel the night air on his body, he strode along the hard, stony ridge of the crest, leaping over the brilliantly moonlit fissures and crevices from mere excess of energy.

At last the rock seemed to fall away on all sides of him at once and, of necessity, he came to a stop. Beneath him a vast inhuman landscape seemed to stretch to a geometrically level horizon. For a long time he stood fascinated by the bright, unlivable prospect and, as the moon moved overhead and the shadows shifted, an irregularity in the vast plain at his feet apparently moved to his right. He became aware of the fact that he was looking at walls only seconds after he knew he was looking at them: walls stretching almost to the base of his present height; sharply defined now, gray like the surface of the moon must be, eaten away by wind and wind-blown sand, eroded at the top by sudden, infrequent rains, it was some time before their regularity became apparent.

The rock quickly gave way to sand, and he descended in long, sliding steps, like some strange desert bird, never quite capable of flight. The sand ended suddenly and, within the walls, the undisturbed dust rose above his ankles and settled over his shoes. Abruptly, he stood still, listening. There was no sound. The walls, three times his height and deathly pale against the night sky, leaned over him, and when he put out his hand, the rough dry mud and rock of their construction was surprisingly real. Gradually, Eric became aware of himself standing in a street that had been empty for a thousand years. The full moon, directly overhead, eliminated shadows, equalizing all in its white, colorless light. For one brief second he was almost frightened, as if it were a dream landscape and he was a child who had stumbled into some ancient part of himself from which he might never escape—no matter how slowly he could run or how silently he could scream. But, as quickly as he shuddered with it, fear left him. He took a few steps through the soft, soundless dust, and another shadowless vista opened itself. He stood at the ancient intersection of two endlessly empty streets, and suddenly it was all clear: the conceived plan, the chosen site, the sustained human effort and, at some unknown, once unpredictable point, the total defeat . . .

Here, truly, was nothing—more so than where the emptiness of the desert was unintruded upon and untouched by the hand of man, more so than where the simple agricultural efforts had simply failed. He walked on. The solid looking, powder soft dust of the dead street rose silently, hovering, moonlit, a few inches above the surface. Nothing. Only the walls which would abruptly end and begin again. No doors or windows. Not an abandoned implement or piece of wood. Not a child to throw a stone and run, or a dog to slink away. Only the spaces where the walls ended, and a new perspective on nothing. Only an infinite silence which would not be contained or shaped.

For no reason, no reason at all, as baseless and as meaningless as the now departed fear, tears rose in him: senseless, unreasonable—as though he had been surprised by music after long silence, as if something had risen in him, unsought and perhaps even unrelated, in a silence between notes, or after the sound had ceased. Tears streamed down his face. His mouth open, his breath came in short, painful sobs. Leaning against the wall, he cried like a child.

But the silence would and did return.

And he became aware of the camera hanging around his neck, and he removed it, freeing it from its soft case, feeling its weight. And then he was motionless again, simply wondering at the thing in his hand: precise, delicate, containing a sparkling round lens in which he now saw himself reflected, and the moon, floating blank and expressionless above his shoulder. And he was surprised at the sound of his own laughter echoing between the walls, and equally surprised by how quickly it died away. Setting the camera in the street before him, he watched the dust rise over it and slowly settle, the metal and the glass apparently aging before his eyes . . .

It was coldest before dawn. Thomas, seeing the first horizontal lines of light in the east, pulled the blanket over his head. Then something made him look again and he stood, holding the blanket about his shoulders and moving his head against the stiffness in his neck. As he faced the light the two pigeons flew out of the well and disappeared on his left. At first the land was black, then gray. Then he forgot about the surface of the earth, for out of the clear, greenish depths of the sky, a red sun was rising, just the sharp, burning curve of it visible at first, the clear yellow rays stabbing out on either side of him as if he were standing at the geographical center of the known world. Then the brightness was upon him, and only the insides of his eyelids were red. Dropping his blanket, his eyes shut tight, he fell on his knees in the soft sand before the sun and bowed his head.

"Oh, God," he said. "Why don't You exist? Why don't You?"

The sun flooded the landscape. The temperature rose immediately. Too cold a second ago, it was already too warm. Turning away from it, Jeff opened his eyes. On the sand before him a beetle carried its cumbersome body about with frequent changes of direction, a funny orange caterpillar uncurled itself, but didn't move. Where . . . oh, yes: the middle of nowhere, the half-dead trees, the gravel piles, his aching hands, untouched Erica a dozen yards away, her back to him. Strange. Strange people. Strange names. Ridiculous. Enough was enough. Empty-handed, but alive! Already he was imagining the Rover bouncing out of the riverbed at the bottom of the wadi, and accelerating beneath him as, at last, he was able to use the higher gears. He could hear the high, contented whine of the engine and feel the smooth surface of the highway beneath him.

Anna opened her eyes. The air was already drying up her mouth and throat. The sun, though barely above the horizon, already seemed larger than the day before. And as it rose higher in the sky, it seemed to roll closer. Or perhaps the earth was tilting towards the sun, and within a few hours they would all slip into the flames. Had anything ever happened to her? She wondered. She had fallen asleep holding the two halves of her discovered stone. Now, mechanically, her hand was fitting them together, allowing them to fall apart, fitting them . . . Five separate people. Yet she felt invisible strands connecting them all. Or did she? She raised her head. Jeff's eyes met hers.

Already awake, Erica stood at the limit of the encampment. The landscape seemed to have only one feature for her: Eric's footprints leading off into the desert as far as she could see, farther, then back again to his still sleeping form. Turning, unaware of the heat, something seemed to catch in her chest, and without waking him, she suddenly knelt in the sand at his side.

The Stone Garden

There is a garden in Kyoto which holds nothing but moss, different mosses. And a few trees. And running water. The young man, who had already flown halfway around the world, stood listening to the sound of running water and watching the winter light move across the soft bright delicate mosses, and the harder darker ones. On the other side of the city there is a garden which holds only stones and sand, and every day the sand is raked clean around the stones. Here there is no running water and when, later that afternoon, the young man stood in that garden, there was perfect silence—unless you could hear the fog moving through the trees outside, or the young man's breathing.

In the center of the city, in a street that looks like an alley and is as quiet, where all the houses stand with their backs to you and silent paper screens slide open to admit you, the young man found an artist who did woodcut prints in sixteen colors. He had done, in several pictures, the story of the bull who disappeared, and three views of the setting sun, and one of the stone garden with the raked sand and the fog or mist moving through the trees, now turning to long lines of rain which bounced a little when they hit the sand.

The young man was somehow struck by the picture in a way he hadn't been by the afternoon's sights. And he stood for several minutes before it, perhaps only experiencing the stone garden for the first time then, and wondering why he never found himself face to face with anything at the time, but only later when it was too late to live anywhere but in his head. Hadn't half the world or, anyway, a thin line on a map of it, already proven empty as a bus ride? At least to eyes that had been child's eyes not so long ago and now, still being young, wanted everything and all at once. He returned from his thoughts only to find that this moment too had slipped by him, and that the artist had been watching him patiently and silently for some time.

"May I buy this one?" the young man asked, and without a word it was prepared and delivered into his hand. And then, as he was about to leave, the artist stopped him, apparently insisting there was someone he must see here and now, since the artist was pointing rapidly and repeatedly straight down. And for some reason, perhaps because he was determined not to miss anything now, the young man gave himself up to this experience and, when the artist finally despaired of making himself understood less forcibly and called a taxi, the young man got in and was carried off.

It began to rain then, soft rain splashing on the roadside as it had on the sand in the picture, and he sat back holding the print rolled in paper beside him on the seat. It felt like a degree in his hand, or like the blank paper roll with the red ribbon they gave you in front of everyone else, the real thing coming later in a brown envelope. He looked out, and having no idea of his destination, found himself enjoying this portion of his trip. The taxi left the city and carried him some distance through trees and rain. There were little plots of cultivated ground now, and peasants and poverty. And finally, there was a square brown house with its back to the road, and an ancient lady, her face not Japanese, who answered his knock and looked at him as he stood under the eaves just out of the cold rain.

"Who are you?" she asked without suspicion, and in good

57

American English. And when he didn't answer, added "Why have you come to me?"

"I don't know," he said.

She looked amused. The taxi had left its motor running. He mentioned the artist in the quiet street. There was a pause. She looked him over again, then asked him where he came from.

"Really! As far as that!" she exclaimed, as if she had just heard that someone she had thought dead was still alive. The taxi shut its motor off. "Halfway round the world," she said quietly, opening the screen wider. "You must come in. You must have tea with me." He entered the unheated house. She closed the screen behind him. "In here. In here." She closed another. "We'll sit here," she said, indicating a table less than a foot off the floor. "You've taken your shoes off? Why don't you take them off now?" she said, sitting on the floor, then lifting a flap that hung from the sides of the table and inserting her legs. "Here. Put your feet in here."

His shoes off, he did as he was told, and wondered what would happen next and for whose sake he had come here and if, after all, the mystery was over: he had been sent to amuse the lady.

"You see," she continued, "though the room is freezing, I am never cold. There is a pot of hot charcoal under here." And he felt the warmth sealed about his legs when he lowered the flap on his side of the table. "Would you like tea?" she asked.

"Yes," he said, and fell silent. He lit a cigarette and looked around the sparsely furnished room. There was hardly more than the mat they sat on, the table and a window looking out at the rain. He didn't feel like amusing anyone. A little Japanese woman came, was addressed in Japanese, left and returned with tea. The lady was as silent as he was until she held the steaming cup in her hand.

"Now we are really warm," she said with twinkling eyes.

Then suddenly her voice dropped. "Now tell me who you are," she said. Amazed at the change in her, he nearly fumbled his cigarette.

"Well, to begin with, I'm not a spy," he managed.

"And I'm not the little old woman who cures you with bones and dice," she said. "There. That takes care of that. So let's not waste an afternoon. Tell me how you see yourself."

He hesitated, then put his cigarette out and decided to answer as well as he could. He began by telling her about the last few months, about that very day.

"Very good," she stopped him, after a few phrases. "I will call you Searcher. I had a dog called Searcher when I was young and beautiful and lived in the Middle West. I was searching myself when I came here. I married a priest. I was young. I've said that," she commented, shaking her head. "My husband is dead," she continued. "But I am too well transplanted ever to return to . . . to your country. Well, what do you want from me, Searcher?"

There was a pause.

"I want to know what you know," he said finally, "what your husband taught you, and what you have learned by yourself."

"I think you must live here many years for that," she said.

"I haven't got many years."

"You have many more than I."

"Not for Kyoto," he said, "not for Japan."

"Where is it you must go?" she asked, and waited. "A few years here might be more memorable than the ones you are about to lead. Think about it. Stay here. It's possible, you know."

"I'll think about it," he said.

"You're lying." There was a silence. "I thought you wanted to know what I know," she said softly. Another silence.

"Can't you just tell me?" He waited. "Tell me where I go from here," he said.

"I'm not a fortune-teller," she said harshly. Then her eyes lit up. "I will tell you something that impressed my husband when he was a young priest, one of the rules." The young man waited. "Do not smoke and urinate at the same time," she said and laughed as if she were remembering her husband's laughter. "There," she added, "you've come halfway around the world for that."

Silence. He did not respond. They sat there while the rain fell and the shadows gathered about the trees. He looked out the window at a massive moss-covered stone which stood in a somehow perfect relation to the house, to the two of them sitting there. He asked her if she had built her house here, if she wanted to live next to that stone for some reason. Yes and no, she said. She did want to live next to it, so they had brought the stone here in a truck just before her husband died. It weighed several tons and looked as if it had always been there.

"It probably always will be now," she said, "for who would bother to truck it away?"

It was time to go. "I think it's a sin to kill time, don't you?" she asked as he put his shoes on. "We don't really have enough left over for killing. At least I don't." She grinned. She seemed meek and harmless again when he stood next to her. Her teeth were dark from years of tea drinking, but her smile was bright anyway and he couldn't help smiling too. He began to say something nice, but she cut him short.

"Do think about it, about staying. Maybe the garden of the stones, maybe the woodcut print in sixteen colors, maybe my big stone were put here just for you."

She told him to come back in a few days, to tell her how he felt then. He agreed to. She stood watching him run the few steps through the rain and slam the taxi door after himself. Small and frail and motionless, she seemed a part of her house then, of her location, almost a part of the landscape he had been travelling through. But, of course, she would be gone soon, and eventually the wood and paper house would follow her. Then only the stone would remain for geologists to wonder about. He tried erasing the slight withered figure in front of the house, but the scene was empty without it. And he wondered how long it would be before he had a picture of this life that he could stand still and look at, and which human faces would appear there and whether, if he erased them, he would be able to put them back. The silent driver smiled when he deposited him at his hotel, and left immediately.

Several days passed, and though the young man's time was limited, he was determined to see everything. Already, in the back of his mind, he saw himself witnessing the low-bowing farewells in the station, and climbing aboard the gleaming streamliner which would whisk him over the snow-covered mountains to Tokyo, and the taxi whisking him to Ginza, where the restaurants were more fabulous than those of Kyoto, and the girls were less expensive and more to the point than the geishas. And he saw one more anonymous taxi proceeding to his plane, the final whisking, and as the itinerary of the immediate future ran through his head, he felt the emptiness of time and the futility of motion, and the huge temples seemed much like airports and he thought, just possibly, that widows might know no more than virgins, and somewhat less than ladies of the night. And, though he stood dutifully before the mighty Buddha who had planted himself, solid and immovable, on twenty-five centuries of incommunicable wisdom, and held to his schedule until Kyoto, seen, no longer held the mystery of the East, and even the silent stone garden did not seem to merit that one return visit, and the woodcut print in

61

sixteen colors lay not quite forgotten in a corner of his hotel room, one day, realizing that seeing all he had seen nothing, he decided that the time had come: the shining train might carry him out of here the following morning.

That night he had dinner in his hotel for the last time. The restaurant was a dark, club-like affair at the end of a long hall behind the lobby. You descended several steps upon entering, and a little red light, perhaps an imitation candle in a glass, flickered at each small round table. As usual, he was practically the only guest. Possibly the Japanese clients at the hotel were familiar with better restaurants, half-hidden on little streets, that he was not aware of, or perhaps they ate at another hour, but it was easiest to eat here. And, having given his order to the English-speaking waitress, he sat back, beginning already the process of saying goodbye to this part of the world and this part of his life. He would take the first train in the morning. He would not bother with another fruitless drive out to the widow's. He would send her a telegram, if necessary, from Tokyo: "Have thought it over. Not suited. Thanks."

Suddenly he felt that he was not alone, and looking up discovered another guest, whom he had not noticed on entering, standing at his side. An American soldier, perhaps his own age, perhaps older, resembling someone he knew, perhaps his brother, was looking frankly and quietly into his eyes as if he too had almost, but not quite, recognized the young man.

"Do I know you?" he asked, and his voice was sincere and quiet too, and the young man had time to notice how trim and well-groomed the soldier was, even to the polish of his buttons and the dapper way he held his officer's cap under his arm.

With a few words they agreed they did not know each other, but that they might as well enjoy each other's company, since there was no one else's. And so they talked and ate, and drank the good Japanese beer, and were amused by the same

62

aspects of Japanese life. There was soft music from somewhere now. And when he looked around again, the young man was surprised to see that somehow the clientele had appeared and taken their places, and were engaged in eating and drinking and talking just as he was.

In fact, he was probably eating and drinking and talking just a little too much for, when he took another look at the soldier, he saw that he had lost some of his neatness, and seemed to be laughing a little too loudly at the young man's humor, and even leering about him at times as if he was flirting grotesquely with someone at another table. They were loud Americans now, he realized, the two of them, for he was talking too loudly as well as too much. But did it matter, since no one knew? And, anyway, it had been so long since he had let himself go and talked with anyone. So the young man excused himself in advance and talked on. He couldn't deny he was holding his audience of one, and finally, bringing his Oriental adventures up to date, he got around to the widow and her cups of tea.

"The priest, her husband, died. God knows when. It might have been twenty years ago. She looked as if she'd been sitting there in the same dress with her feet tucked under the table for all twenty of them."

The soldier chuckled appreciatively. "And," the young man added, in what he realized later must have been loud understatement, "the only wisdom she had to impart was 'Don't smoke when you pee.' "

The advice must have sounded much more humorous now than it had been helpful when he heard it, for the disheveled soldier was guffawing loudly and the young man, feeling very funny, was joining in and leaning successfully back in his chair, allowing his eyes to rove over the people who had finally deigned to eat there. And it was just then—later he would remember the

63

sense of looking out of his own sparkling eyes over his open mouth—that he met the quiet gaze of the widow herself.

He swallowed. He blinked. He shook his head. She was still there, conversing softly with Japanese friends. Her words were inaudible. She was not looking at him now, of course, and perhaps she never had.

"It's her!" he said, turning back.

"It's who?" asked the soldier, raising his eyebrows.

"The widow," he said, his voice almost a stage whisper.

The soldier smiled, but didn't say anything.

"Do you think she heard me?"

"You were talking pretty loudly," said the soldier.

The young man glanced at his plate. It would be foolish to allow a little incident like this, that may or may not have occurred, to upset him. Seconds later, he was in the washroom, feeling hot and cold, lighting a cigarette with trembling fingers and standing at the urinal to give himself a reason for being there. Suddenly his intestines were leaping, and he just barely managed to make it to the metal cubicle and slam the door, already holding himself painfully in a sitting position and hating the awkward hole between the footrests.

Swaying forward weakly, his forehead came to rest against the cool metal door, and images of Tokyo flashed behind his eyes: weird nighttime settings, men dressed as women, young girls lining the Ginza streets, women giggling and drinking whiskey-colored water at your expense, and one horrible horseshoe-shaped bar where the lady came swinging around overhead, planting her pink shoes on either side of your drink, and it was your pleasure to reach up and in. He was ready to promise anything, a new life, when the spasms, mental and physical, passed as rapidly as they had begun and he pushed his head away from the door, maintaining his balance on his throbbing legs alone.

"Are you okay?" The smooth voice of the soldier just outside. Apparently he was his suave self again.

"Yes," the young man answered impatiently.

"The waitress wants to know if you intend to pay your bill."

"Of course I intend . . ." he began angrily. "Wait, I can't go back in there. Will you . . . ?"

"Certainly," said the soldier. "Just slide it under the door."

The young man, cursing the Orient for its lack of toilets you could sit on, finally managed to reach his wallet.

"I'll be lucky if I can walk when I get out of here," he said, throwing his money out.

"Sit on your heels," said the soldier softly, and left.

All was quiet. The storm was past. The experience, thank God, was over. Shakily standing, his eyes fell on the spat-out cigarette lying forlorn and extinguished on the wet tiles. He sighed. He waited a moment by the open window, breathing the cool air of the night, and returned to his hotel room. He never saw the soldier again and the bill, he found out later, had been paid. That night the young man decided to return to the widow's as originally agreed.

"Just one question," he insisted the next morning when he saw her. "Are you a witch?"

She laughed. His taxi had taken him out on schedule through a thin rain, and now stood waiting under a tree, its engine off. She didn't say anything, gesturing him in again and making him sit with her again with their legs under the table. There was nothing in her manner to suggest that she had seen or heard him as recently as the previous night. And her eyes, which never left his, were kind.

"You kept your word," she said. "I like that." He began to open his mouth. "No, don't say anything," she continued. "I've thought it over too. I don't believe you're suited." She

65

smiled. "But just remember, young man, one thing at a time."

The tea appeared. She did not seem inclined to say any more.

"One thing at a time?" he said.

She poured some of the scalding liquid into her cup.

"First life, then art," she said.

"Then art," he repeated.

"There's no God as far as you're concerned," she said. "Now go. Be humble. Work. And keep your mouth shut."

She sipped her cup of steaming tea. She looked at her stone. She looked at him.

At the door he turned to face her.

"Goodbye now," she said before he could speak, and she smiled her bright tea-stained smile and held out her small warm hand.

That afternoon the train carried him over the mountains.

Inga

Inga liked little men. Mark was the exception.

The type is not unknown: hamster-eyes, they tilt their heads against her armpit. She walks with her arm about their shoulders. They learn from her that this is all right, that that is all right, and the other thing too. They float serene in their knowledge.

Mark was different.

August 17, 1983

> Dear Mark,
> I know. Even the envelope is a surprise. After all these years. No excuse. You have your life. But. Could you come?
>
> Inga

His wife drove him to the airport.

"No explanations."

He nodded. "I'll be back."

"I know."

Inga, 1960, a girl with all the colors on a once white blouse, pigment in her fingers. Inga is nearly six feet high. Hair that only begins to thin as it reaches her waist, eyes that receive and hold. Her breasts are small against the fullness of her chest.

Inga wears jeans, even into the water. She thinks her legs are too strong. Inga's English sentences break. Break on the shores of a wonderful hesitancy. Her Dutch is not much better.

Anneka, 1960. Anneka is a green and bending reed, a dancer's dancer with hardly any hair between her legs. She knows no bodily pleasure. She has never been known to eat. She has no behind and her legs move all of a piece, toes out.

She walks right out of his life like that. She knows. She knows it is Inga.

Inga at the airport. Summer, 1983. He saw her through the glass. His smile, unaware of itself, bounced back at him. Carelessly leaving fingerprints, he found his way to her.

Inga. Eyes unchanged. Thickness of hair unchanged; depth of shading gone in places, another color finding its way to the end.

A café. He ordered coffee because the word was simple. His bag pressed against his knee. Her sentences broke at his feet.

"It was good of you. I wouldn't have."

Her fingers on his sleeve, her hair drifting out. Without knowing it, she was letting him look into her eyes.

1960. The sisters have a place in San Francisco. On Fell. Above the Fillmore and before the days of Haight-Ashbury. A painted floor. Two mattresses. One for Inga, one for Anneka. They are two on each. Inga and her little man on one, Mark and Anneka on the other. Anneka tells him there is not much on her dancer's chest. He does not complain. She tells him she has not yet found pleasure, but she doesn't mind if he does. Two mattresses. His body in one, his heart in the other.

"There's a time. For everything," she said, her voice unchanged.

68

"For everything," he repeated. "Yes," he was being witty; "if only we knew when it was."

"We do. We just don't know. When it is."

He was nodding, thinking he understood. He was looking at her, suspecting he didn't.

"I have been rereading. Van Gogh's letters," she said. "I have been thinking. Is it worth it? Well, is it? Of course, there are other lives. That destroy."

In Virginia she walks into the sea. With her jeans on. It is the summer of 1960. They have crossed the country together. Mark stands behind, well out of the water, knowing what is on the other side. No, he knows nothing. It is an afternoon, ten years later, the words never spoken. No.

The café was filling up. A thin layer of smoke settled between them.

They found their way down dark canals. Bright lights, impenetrable shadows. Her face vivid, close; her face gone.

She wasn't ready to talk.

At a small bar the liqueur glass was filled to the brim and left standing. A few stylish men and women, hands behind them, bent for the first obligatory sip. A momentary silence. A different age. The return to this one.

It was a warm night. Mark and Inga stood outside. Mark wondered why there was no smell of the sea.

Inga returned her glass.

"And now. Where would you like . . ."

A tour. He thought of closed museums, of people lost, unable to find each other.

"Mark. Are you listening?"

Beneath the darkness of her hair, he caught her look.

He finds her eyes. It is their first morning. 1960. Arizona or New Mexico. A cheap square room. The Morris Minor sleeps outside. Los Angeles is behind them. She is Mark's. For a summer. He is not yet aware of the limitation.

1983. City of art, city of concentric circles. Tobacco, wine, china and preserves. They approached the Dam. The sound of voices was a not-so-distant sea.

Two people, one suitcase.

"Here the Nazis. Got their Jews," said Inga.

"Did they?" asked Mark, trying to remember.

"In Italy. In France. Some got away. Here. It was different."

Mark noticed a man behind them. They turned a corner. He turned too. Without hurrying, he was closer. He seemed to raise his eyebrows slightly. His eyes looked into Mark's with genuine interest.

"We are being followed."

"Pay. No attention."

"Why not?"

"Drugs."

Mark looked again. "But why . . . has he chosen us?"

"Why does anybody. Choose anything?"

1960. A cafeteria. The roar of dumped trays. A girl with all the colors about her wrists. A man's shirt to keep the paint from her jeans. She speaks of Van Gogh, exile, religion. She speaks to a young man smaller than herself, to a girl so thin Mark does not recognize her as the same flesh.

"Theo's wife," she is saying. "Her life. For Vincent's work. Yet she sought. Theo in the letters."

Anneka is pushing a broccoli stem with her fork. The head is gone, though she never saw it rise to her mouth.

"She kept the record. For her son," says Inga. "That he might judge. If she had used her life. Wisely."

Murmurs, seemingly, of one voice. Sounds of moving feet. Who were they? Moluccans? Jews? Did they know each other? Did they keep track?

They were taken up. Of necessity they took each other's hands. They moved against the current. They drifted away from the light and back.

"Are you all right?"

"Are you?"

"I thought perhaps you weren't."

"Not me."

Turning, turning, they spoke of other things. They were in the center. Around them good roads led to Delft, Bruges, a sea of tulips, sand. But they were here now. And some lived whole lives in Amsterdam. They married, raised their children, died.

The cafeteria is behind them. The fog is in. Mark has an address in his pocket. He turns to watch them go.

Inga's legs are strong. Anneka's are thin and cold. They will carry her when her one mention on Dutch radio is long forgotten.

Inga has her arms around the young man's shoulders. Mark has to stand straight to be as tall as Inga, but he doesn't need that.

A fresh roll of fog covers them. They are gone. Trees disappear. So does he.

"And tomorrow," says Inga. "I can borrow a Volvo. We will drive. To the Kroller-Müller. There are Van Goghs. A sculpture garden. Dunes. They anchored the dunes. Now they are beginning. To let them move again."

"And the day after tomorrow?"

"We'll come back."

"And then?"

"Then we'll drive. North."

"North."

Inga stopped them, Mark's hand in hers, to look in that direction. People swirled.

"We'll stand," said Inga. "On the shore. At the Wadden Zee. We'll look out."

"At what?"

"Islands."

"And then?"

"Then you'll go home."

1960. The first afternoon. Two mattresses seem ready to be thrown out. There is no chair. Inga stands awkwardly. Anneka returns, thin and showered from the dance. Three silent figures.

The second night. Two mattresses, a candle in a bottle. They are a circle round the flame. Mouth open, gratefully, Mark receives the wine from Inga's lips. Humbly, he releases it between Anneka's.

Later, in the dark, he holds a thin and silent body. Inga also holds a silent form. She will not speak to Mark.

1983. They stopped. The silence spread around them.

A man in shirt sleeves told a sailor to move on. The sailor feinted at his stomach, hit him in the face.

A window opened. A woman with too much makeup spoke a flat English. Her terms were not agreed to. A man, his face never visible, moved on.

"Let's go to bed," said Mark.

Inga's head moved slowly up and down. He saw the lights of a hotel behind her.

"Here?" he asked.

They were walking again. The streets were brighter. The whores sat in lighted windows, scenes of a wonderful domesticity behind them.

They neared the hotel.

"I don't. Have my passport," said Inga. "You can come. Home."

1960. Anneka is gone, flying to an audition which is only the beginning of an end. Mark is driving Inga to the boat.

He sits on a park bench sketching the old Morris. He doesn't mind. He can wait. He left her at the little man's. In Pasadena or Hollywood. It doesn't matter, he can find it. They will take pictures of each other getting out of the shower. He doesn't care. They bought the car together, she and Mark. They sat in the front seats. They looked out through the windshield.

Into the night. A road he knows has no end crosses Texas, descends the Mississippi, enters and leaves the old South. It touches the furthest sea. But they are in the desert, alone with the gods of Morris Garage. Their prayers touch on small personal matters like fuel pumps.

Success. It is ticking like a clock. Then . . . They know by the silence. They are only drifting.

He is out. The hood is up. He is in. A hundred yards, two. He is out. In.

Inga sits at his side. If she is still saying her goodbyes, she is doing it without words. He has not even lifted her sweater yet.

Silence. Drifting. Out. In. A recurring act. They roar together. Inga doubles in her seat. Mark dances by the side of the road.

An hour later, the same routine. Only he has lost his audience. Inga is in Hollywood or Los Angeles. Mark is in hell.

After the fuel pump it is the tires, each in turn releasing its burden of trapped air. The emergency brake is a loose, useless lever in his hand. First gear is a slow stirring of metal bits. But the desert is behind them. Her goodbyes are behind her.

Days. Top down, they descend the map. Along the great river, a high continuous arch of trees, the smell of water, their hands together between the seats.

Nights. Under the thickness of that hair, his fingers discover one eye, then another. He falls asleep on her.

On. Second gear is a soft pudding of sound. Third is their deliverance.

Polished brass. Polished wood. Deep, silencing carpets. Clothes on a chair. Linen. Numbers that glowed in the dark. He watched the clock, trying to believe it.

A movement. Inga was on her elbow, thinking. Mark was looking at walls he could not see.

"Would you like. To meet my boys?"

"We've already met."

"They were. Children."

"What are they now?"

He waited for an answer, then forgot to. He had a feeling it might be three a.m.

New Orleans, the French cemetery. They climb the wall. They read the headstones and say nothing. No one here is over twelve. Who are they? Whose are they? They have names.

New York. The little car is gone. They eat at one more counter. Inga stands on the deck of a white Dutch ship. She is twenty-one.

"How long. Have you got?" she asked.

He remembered his ticket.

"Twenty-one days."

"Would you like. To go somewhere?"

"Inga. Let me sleep. Just a few minutes."

A movement. Her hair covered him.

Was this how she held them, her boy-men? No wonder there was no room for her sons. He closed his eyes. He opened them.

Another present vanished into another past.

1971. Ten years ago he drove her east. She stepped into the sea. She's been to Belgium now, married and bred. He never meets this first husband, though he sees his picture. He is standing next to her. He has 'Artist' written all over him. Mark estimates his height precisely at four-nine.

He has those eyes. She can't resist them. Mysteriously, he fathers two healthy sons upon her. Just as mysteriously, he is gone.

1971. American bombs are falling. Mark knows where. He doesn't want to think about it.

A cold pier in Rotterdam. Chance has brought him here, and a disabled freighter. He stops before a phone, a miniscule Dutch dime in his hand. A seagull walks on the ice.

"Is it you?"

"You know. It is. Have you come? To see me?"

He lies. He is on his way. A flat landscape flings itself at the train. An Indonesian couple sits across from him.

"You are American?" asks the husband.

"Yes."

"Would we be welcome in America?" asks the wife.

Inga on the platform. Mark is on it too. Has she grown slightly or has he shrunk? In spite of the cold she wears jeans. No, they are not wet to the knees.

The smallest of small cars waits. It appears to have rolled over many times. The engine churns, apparently dies and churns again.

Surprise: Inga has embraced a character who already has one hand on his M.D. This doctor-to-be smiles through a windshield.

The doors are open. The pedal is to the floor. Mark is on his knees across the back seat.

"I should be celebrating." The doctor's English is correct. "I have just passed my exams."

He slows. Mark is sitting now. The eyes in the rear view mirror examine his. The car surges. Mark is looking at the roof.

"I should be celebrating," the doctor says again. "Then you came."

"What have I got to do with it?"

"Where would you like to go?" he asks, ignoring this. "What would you like to see?"

"I'm not a tourist," says Mark.

"Oh yes you are."

Inga looks at Mark, entreaty in her eyes. But he lunges away as the car rounds a corner and bounces over the curb.

He braces his foot against the opposite door. It flies open. The roof flies open. On the next turn the door closes.

"Would you like to see an exhibit?" The doctor.

They skid to a stop, Mark's head between theirs. Inga reaches up to re-attach the roof.

He follows them between the deKoonings and Kandinskis. He notes the doctor-to-be is not very large. He has the eyes of a Dutch mouse. His fingers are translucent. He disappears behind oversize doors.

"How is Anneka?" asks Mark. "And you. Are you happy?" They pause before a famous canvas: *black on black*. "Are you painting?" he asks. "Are you still painting?"

The little man is relieving himself. He is washing his hands. He is coming up behind her.

Inga's lips move at last.

"No. No more."

"No more what?" he asks.

Anneka's American husband stands before Mark. He is learning Dutch so he will never again have to speak his own language. Anneka stands in the shadows, this man's baby against her breast.

Composed, a picture, she looks at Mark with large eyes. She raises her hand.

At Inga's a man and woman have come to dinner. They live in a small apartment near the Rijksmuseum. Inga has arranged for Mark to spend the night with them. He cannot stay here. She, the woman, is going to leave the man.

Jacques. Frans. Inga's half-Belgian boys are seven and nine. They do not speak English. Frans's eyes are Inga's, Inga's alone, or Mark's. His hair is hers.

It is decided: Frans will be an artist.

Mark shows him how two, silently, can reflect each other. He faces him. Slowly he raises his foot. Frans has the idea. His small foot floats from the floor, a genuine reflection. He raises

77

his hand. Mark raises his. They offer each other a tragic, yet restrained farewell. Less than tragic, perhaps, with one foot in the air. Inga smiles from the door.

Frans raises his face to Mark, Mark lowers his to Frans. Frans turns, Mark turns. And suddenly, crudely, Frans sticks out his behind. They are walking away from each other. Inga is laughing. Mark looks out the window.

Inga is on the telephone. Mark stands next to her in the hall. It is his only chance. He speaks softly, quickly, the first words that come to him.

"I'm stronger than you are."

"Are you?"

She is speaking Dutch again. He cannot think of anything else. He will that night.

A small, spotless apartment near the Rijksmuseum, home of the soon-to-be-divorced. They are on the couches; Mark is in the bed. The bed is full of tears. There is a soft insurmountable ridge down the middle and a still, body-shaped pool to either side. One mirrors the wall, one the door. Mark has a foot in each.

Earlier, at Inga's where he cannot stay, man and woman take turns discussing their impasse. In English, which is kind. The good doctor keeps their glasses full. Inga and Mark, the lighted scene between them, listen and do not listen.

A phrase comes. He whispers it now.

He knows they are lying awake in the next room.

Morning. The woman sleeps facing the door. The man sets two cups of coffee on the counter. Mark stands beside him. They drink facing the wall.

He runs beside Mark carrying his bag. The train is there. Mark steps in. He waits for the door to close between them. He knows he should say something.

"I hope . . ."

They are the wrong words. The doors close.

1983. Walls he could not see, numbers that glowed.

Inga was gone. Mark ran after.

No.

A thin layer of smoke settled between them. Slowly it changhed its shape.

"I married. An artist," she said.

"The wrong one," suggested Mark.

"The wrong. Doctor too," said Inga.

She was laughing, her hair drifting out.

It was a warm night. He wondered why there was no smell of the sea. Inga returned her glass.

"And now . . ."

Another tour, this time without the doctor. He thought of people disappearing.

"Mark. Are you listening?"

"Yes, yes. Let's go. Perhaps we'll stumble across your son."

He wished he had said it differently.

Bright lights, impenetrable shadows.

"We are being followed."

"Pay. No attention.'

"Why not?"

"Drugs."

He opened his mouth. He closed it. He walked beside her with bowed head.

They stood together in the square. The suitcase was taken away, their clothes. Thousands, thousands stood beside them.

And in the distance, converging, the sound of trucks.

No.

Inga stood beside him. She seemed to be looking. He too saw the collapsed form in the doorway, the amazing hair . . .

Inga moved more quickly than Mark. She was crouching, kneeling; the name was on her lips, the head was in her hands.

"Frans. Frans."

She raised it. Wrong man.

She stood. Mark took her hand. They walked all night.

No.

He stood. He wandered naked to the kitchen.

"You haven't. Changed much."

"What are you doing?"

"Cooking. For you."

Mark opened the wine, absurd in his human form. He found the shower. He followed the smell of food back to Inga.

A flickering light. The kitchen table was too small. Their knees touched.

He wondered whatever happened to the soon-to-be-divorced. He realized Anneka's name would not be heard this night. He knew that Jacques was gone, and Frans.

Frans was nine, bending at the waist to mock him. Now Frans had found one of the lives that destroy . . .

"You think. Too much," said Inga. "Have you. Got children?" she asked.

He tried to think of an answer. He took her hand and raised

it to his mouth. He got down on his knees and put his head
in her lap.

What? What was this? He never knew.

He closed his eyes.

He wondered what happened that year in New Orleans. He
wondered why the children died.

"We will. Go away," said Inga.

He looked up. Inga was looking at her walls.

"You have to. Be there. When you're needed," she said.
"Not when you're not. You have to. Let go."

Mark looked away.

"Then gather up again," she continued. "Then. Let go."

He held her thighs. He pressed assurance into her knees.
But there was no strength in her legs, and not much keeping
her in the chair.

The smell of coffee. A neat Dutch breakfast. He sprinkled
chocolate on his bread.

The Volvo was on its way. It was bright, solid. In it they
would be a couple. They would strap themselves in.

"Inga."

"What?"

"Why did you say you wouldn't have. Come?"

He was beginning to talk like her.

"I don't know. I don't think. I would have. Ever. Anneka
might have."

"Anneka?"

The Ice Forest

A formless sky somehow in motion, a grayness sliding vaguely from one corner of the window to the other. And just visible through the dry spotted glass, an iron bollard and a cable stretching up the side of the now empty ferry. He remembered seeing the *quai* swarming with travellers, hearing their laughter, their excitement . . .

"I'm wondering . . ." she began.

Out of the corner of his eye her voice seemed to be rising from a battlefield of breadcrumbs, from her empty cup. She paused, and he was aware of the cold beyond the *café* window taking hold of his ankles and his wrists.

"I'm wondering if I mean nothing to you or if you mean nothing to me," she continued.

He laughed, suddenly looking at her. She wasn't laughing. He glanced around. *Le garçon*, a statue in faded black and faded white, stood out of hearing near the *caisse.* There was no one else. He twisted his own empty cup in its saucer.

"We have been together precisely one day," he began.

"Yes, one day!" she interrupted. Her eyes became brighter and her teeth showed when she said "day."

For a moment they stared at each other, their thoughts and feelings completely different. Then his eyes twinkled. He conceived an almost cruel, yet undeniably funny remark, a wild overstatement of her relative youth and immaturity. He cleared his throat.

"Everything will look better when . . ." he began quietly.

"When?" she interrupted again.

He looked around, then leaned closer, just holding lightly to the rim of his cup. But the rising witticism stuck somewhere in his chest. And again they just looked at each other, her eyes filling with tears.

"When we're further into the country," he said gently. "You'll see." He sat back. "I thought I'd let the hurried ones tear for Paris. Did you like your *café au lait?*"

There was a pause. She looked down at her empty cup.

"I don't think I tasted anything," she said without looking up.

"Well, there's a cure for that. Would you care for another, *mademoiselle?*" he asked gallantly.

"Perhaps one," she said, drawing herself up, elegant, ladylike.

He raised his hand slightly and the symphony in gray, gray on gray, sprang to life, flipping a gray dishtowel over a gray sleeve with some style.

He watched her swigging off her coffee, the tears not dry on her cheeks, yet smiling. He asked for and received the last swallow, the milk foam on his moustache already causing her to suppress a laugh. She stood up suddenly, her slim hips and legs rising above the table like a vision. Out in the cold she condescended to take his arm, and he had to hurry to keep up with her. In front of the car rental agency the little *deux chevaux* waited almost humanly for them, its blank face neutral like that of a dog willing to go anywhere and do anything with them. She nearly skipped ahead when she saw it, laughing.

Turning the key he hummed a little to give himself courage.

"Are you going to sing to me?" she asked.

"Someday."

He crept out of town, one eye on the unfamiliar controls. From time to time she took his hand, and from time to time, nervously, he took it back.

"Oh, look!" she pointed brightly. "We're almost doing a hundred."

"Don't scare me like that," he said. "I thought it was about to blow up or something. That's a hundred kilometers we're almost doing," he added.

"Do you always drive like this?" she asked.

"More or less."

"I thought only . . ." She looked at him, her eyes laughing. "Oh," she said, "I wasn't going to say 'only funerals.' " Her eyes closed and he wondered what she had been going to say. "Now I'm just making it worse, aren't I?" she asked. "I think we should just accept the fact that our ages differ, don't you?"

"I think that would be a good idea," he said.

They continued in silence, though the little car was not silent. The road ran straight between immense fields. There were no trees. It seemed he was already tired. He didn't like this early rising. Mentally he cursed the ferries, the tiny cabins with their bright lights. He pictured his own home at this hour, the rooms, the furniture, the goings and the comings this first morning without him.

"I don't think I like France," she said suddenly.

"You haven't seen very much of her."

"It's very barren and there're no colors," she said.

"Perhaps it will snow."

"I'd like that. I like snow."

In a village he parked carefully in front of a small *épicerie* and took her inside to buy a bottle of wine and a camembert. After inquiry he drove straight to the nearest *boulangerie*, where he ran in and came out with the longest *baguette* he could find. He handed it to her through the car window so audaciously that she slapped it in mock anger before allowing it in the car. Then she allowed him in too and they continued as slowly as before.

Avoiding Paris the roads are smaller, less direct, and they join each other at odd angles, often only after you have followed still another road, in an altogether different direction, for a little while. After a few hours he felt he had been driving weeks, playing checkers on the map of France. On a lonely rise, on a road he wasn't even sure was the right one, between two great expanses of black mud which were probably farms, he drove the *deux chevaux* onto the shoulder and turned it off. In the unfamiliar silence it was a moment before they felt the wind buffeting the car and the metal cooling around them. Suddenly they were starving. And soon they found themselves covered with breadcrumbs, their fingers stinking from the cheese, which probably should have been saved for the following summer, and forcing the cork into the bottle with the screwdriver from the tool kit, he somehow managed to bathe one ankle in ice-cold wine.

Everything amused her, the last incident most of all. And suddenly they were freezing. He started up the car and turned the heater on. He felt sleep creeping up his legs from his warming feet. She allowed him to brush the crumbs off her. Then he just rested his hands lightly on her breasts and she watched him peacefully.

"When did we decide to run off like this?" she asked after a few seconds.

"Didn't we meet on the boat?" he asked innocently.

85

She looked at him blankly. "Wasn't it London?"

"It may have been. I thought it was New York," he added.

"You bought me a drink, didn't you?" she asked.

"Did I? Oh, yes. Dubonnet, wasn't it?"

"Was it? I thought it was Pepsi."

When she laughed her white teeth showed and her hair slipped softly over her neck. With his fingertips he just touched her white teeth. When she spoke her lips moved against his fingers. He couldn't understand a word. In fact her voice was coming to him over an infinite distance. His head was against the back of the seat. He closed his eyes. His hand slipped down her body. Much, much later it seemed a voice, his own, was whispering something in his ear about carbon monoxide and he jumped.

"Oh, well, how long was I asleep?" he asked, quickly sitting up, running his hand over his face.

"About a minute," she said.

In the dark he didn't know the name of the town. And he didn't want to look at the map, not even once more. Suddenly finding themselves in city streets, they had decided to stop. There was the *Hôtel du Chemin* or the *Hôtel des Voyageurs* or whatever, beckoning, and they entered. Almost immediately they were packed together in a miniature elevator, a uselessly high, narrow cage in the middle of the stairwell which seemed to have been designed for a lonely skier. Their bags were packed between them by a man of indefinite age, but definite odor, wearing what appeared to be a uniform from the Franco-Prussian War, who then joined them.

All at once they leapt about a foot, then settled for a painfully slow upward grind accompanied by a high-pitched, desperate scream. The battlefield odor rose with them. At practically the same moment, unseen, she managed to cover her nose as he raised his hands to his ears. Immediately their bags crashed to the floor, but it didn't matter. The cage had shuddered to a halt as violently as it had begun. They stepped out *au bel étage*. Later, a cold empty dining room, tasteless food mixed with memories of the uniform, the odor; facts which might all, somehow, be related, if he had had the energy.

And love, yes love. And in the silence before sleep they found they were no longer strangers. And in a state in which he didn't know if he were asleep or awake, whole countries, warm and green, seemed to be passing directly underneath him. In the middle of the night he awoke, finding himself holding one of her small breasts and tears running silently down his face, tears it seemed he had no particular right to, tears which he did not understand. Then the trucks began to pass on the cobblestones, one after the other, heavy trucks going somewhere, perhaps to a new war, he thought, in which we shall all die. The lights swept across the room. The windows shook in their frames. The door, the walls, the bed shook too. She slept.

They had expected snow all day, yet at dusk it still had not fallen. The damp countryside and darkening fields seemed abandoned like the highway, waiting. It was difficult to see, to tell the dark paving from the darker verge, and he only became aware of the squint on his face after it had been there several minutes. He fumbled with the lights, got them on, but the approaching night seemed to absorb their brightness and he could see no better than before.

On a curve a small white concrete sign came suddenly into sight pointing off to the left, a small road rising behind it. But just as he was trying to make out the letters *"Le D . . ."* a big Citroën screeched past him on the curve and, just as suddenly, an oncoming truck appeared in front of him and, angered by

87

this maneuver, feigned a turn directly in front of the speeding Citroën. This so angered the driver of the Citroën that he stopped, jumped out cursing and then, in spite of his wife's pleas, jumped back in, his tires throwing up the dirt as he turned to speed after the truck. It had all happened so quickly that they had come to a stop in the middle of the road to watch it. Now the highway was empty again, silent and dark. They had only to drive a few feet and turn left at the sign.

Lurching into the empty central square in first gear, it seemed the *deux chevaux* had lost one of its horses on the ascent. They stopped. There was hardly a light to be seen, not a restaurant, not a hotel. He got out of the car and tried to stamp a little life into his legs. It was much colder. A freezing wind seemed to be pouring into the square from all sides. Arm in arm, their clothing clutched about them, they struggled up one dark street after another. At last they discovered a smaller adjoining square, containing the large stone *église*, a light bulb more often off than on, swinging on its length of wire above the entrance. In the hope that someone inside could guide them, together they pulled open the oaken door with its iron fastenings, which at once slammed heavily behind them.

Inside they discovered a new darkness, a windless cold. Around them unlit stone walls mounted into invisibility. Across a seemingly impassable gulf a single candle burned in front of the distant altar. Attempting to find their way forward, she somehow plunged her hand in icy holy water, he kicked a collection box. A door opened at the sound. An old woman looked in and quickly disappeared. They waited for her to reappear, and when she didn't, they stepped out once more into the wind. Once more under the swinging, blinking light bulb, this time they discovered a hotel facing them directly across the street.

Two sets of creaky doors, one with a stained glass pattern,

readily admitted them. The hall was cold and barely lit. As their eyes adjusted they noticed a sideboard flanking one wall with a dignified display of old china. A staircase rose before them hung with an ascending series of oil paintings, all in golden frames, all apparently holding the still, perfect light of calm northern interiors. The cleanliness was palpable, as if each morning a steaming bucket stood where they stood now.

A woman appeared from behind the stairs. Almost without a word she led them up and up to a spotless room, turned the handles of the radiators under two small windows set deeply into the thick wall, and left. It was cold. The water in the sink was cold, too cold to wash with. The overhead light was so bright they turned it off. Their coats still on, invisible to each other, they sat on the large inset sills. If not heat, there was at least sound in the radiators. There was the sound of the wind in the dark streets too. It seemed to be rushing between the squares, around the church, and back past the hotel. A streetlight came on. Dinner would be in three hours.

"Can you hear me over there?"

"Yes. Can you hear me?" he asked after a moment.

"Yes. What do you think happened?"

There was a moment of silence.

"Happened?" he asked, barely audible.

"Yes. To the car and the truck. I'm going to walk back down the road and see what happened. Coming?"

There was no answer though she stood up energetically, pulling on her coat, and went to stand in front of the other window. He was asleep, his head against the cold wall. She touched his cheek, cold and rough, with her whole hand and without moving, he opened his eyes. She didn't know which of them smiled first and, instead of walking down the road, she crawled in the window with him. He put his head across her thighs. In the street the occasional car passed. Slowly the lights played around the room: in one window, over the ward-robe, the sink with its tiny mirror, out the other window. Just so, she thought, just so. She ran her hand over his head and he was asleep.

Candlelight. Wine. The dining room not completely empty. Our eyes are deep pools of silence, she thought, sometimes a breath of doubt moves across them, sometimes something bright shoots deep within them and we laugh. What's this? There are so many tastes. Don't tell me. I know. Why are you smiling like that? Can you read my thoughts? No! Don't look away. Don't laugh. All right, laugh. You are beautiful too. Especially your mouth, yes, your lips. Do you mind my look-ing at them? You are one of my tastes too. But why are there tears in our eyes, tears in our eyes at the same moment?

"Can you tell me that?" she asked.

"What?"

"Why there were tears in our eyes at the same moment."

After the dining room, in the darkness on the first stair, she leaned back against him, rubbing the back of her head against his face. Nearly losing her balance, she pulled herself away and pushed the plastic button on the wall. High above them, the top floor lights came on.

"We have so little time," she said with great seriousness, "before the lights go out."

She started climbing, deliberately lifting one foot, then the other. Her hand on the bannister guiding her, she observed the pictures on the wall, their perspectives seeming to change as she rose higher. It was strange to be in one building looking into the interiors of others. It was strange to be able to re-member such food, such wine, with her tongue, almost with her teeth. All at once she turned, looking down at him two steps beneath her.

90

"You were going to sing to me!" she said.

"Me?"

"You."

Suddenly he spread his arms and began some wonderful old song she never heard of. Then the lights went out, she collapsed laughing in his arms and he nearly fell.

"You . . . tenor!" she said.

"Could be worse," he said, hanging onto the bannister.

Then he regained his balance and tightened his arms around her.

"Are we always going to be this happy?" she asked against his mouth.

"Always."

They laughed again, nearly falling together. Moments later she found another plastic button glowing feebly in the dark. Pressing it, far beneath them she saw the ground floor lights come on. Above them the stairs still ascended into darkness.

"You have ninety seconds, sir," she said.

"Ce n'est pas beaucoup."

"You may hold on if you like," she said. "That way I know I won't lose you."

They began the last flight. This time they almost made it.

Later, a miracle: in the darkness of the room in the middle of the night—hot water, the rim of the bidet warm and comfortable. Warmth from the radiators too. He stood naked by the window, his knees pressed against the warm metal. Through washing herself, she sat watching him. Later she went to stand beside him. He turned to look at her. The pale light from the street illuminated them both. White, incongruous bodies, separate in time too.

"Were Adam and Eve so different?" one of them asked.

"God only knows," said the other.

91

And they smiled at the picture of themselves banished and fleeing.

He stood behind her, his arms surrounding her nakedness. The wind was softer now, colder, gently pushing through the streets. The single bulb blinked fitfully over the doors to the church. He held her more closely. Child in a woman's body, he thought, woman in a child's. I will never let anyone hurt you. Never. Then the silence of the night included them, and even the stone buildings of the village, having somehow fed, now slept.

It began to snow and the snow turned to rain during the night, and in the morning even the rain had stopped. The fields in the distance were dark and empty, the streets of the village were glistening and cold. Full of bread and coffee they pushed their way out through both sets of creaky doors and hurried along the sidewalk. The sky was low and shapeless, a gray mass hurrying south over their heads. Throwing in of bags, slamming of doors. It was still early morning as the little car wound down the road to the highway, stopped, and leapt noisily forward, turning south.

She leaned over the back of the seat to read the sign as it would appear coming from the other direction. He watched her out of the corner of his eye, thinking she should sit down and fasten her seat belt. She sat down.

"We will never be here again, will we?" she asked after a moment.

He glanced at her. "Probably not."

"Never," she said more quietly. "At least I got the name of the place," she added.

"Oh?" he asked. "What is it?"

After a moment he realized she had no intention of telling

him, and he smiled and even managed to speed up a little so she wouldn't become bored in the tunnel of dormant trees. Southward, ever southward, he thought. Instinctive, like birds. But are there really any new worlds, he wondered? And where are they? On a candlelit tablecloth, in a mysterious wine-red bottle, in a young woman's body or in a glimpse of country he had never seen before traversed by an empty road? And why were some scenes empty and dead? Perhaps the same scene in a different light. Beyond these hands on the wheel, he thought, what is there? What really is out there, he wondered, in front of me?

They passed a truck loading big cans of milk from a platform. They continued through small fields, past stone houses and rusty gates, over mud and manure tracked out by the cows, by the cows, *par les vaches.* Was he tired already? He had lost some of his speed, he knew, and it was such an effort to get it back.

"What are you thinking?" she asked suddenly.

He straightened his back and pressed a little more heavily on the accelerator.

"Well?" she asked quickly.

"I'm wondering," he began, "I'm wondering if it's still possible to go everywhere and do everything."

"Is it?"

"I always thought it was," he said.

"You know what I'm thinking?" she asked.

"No."

"I'm thinking one of these cars coming at us is going to have my father and your wife in it."

He smiled at the picture. "I wonder how the two of them ever got together," he said, waking up.

"They're both going to see us at the same time," she continued. "Their heads will turn together. They'll screech to a stop like that car last night. Then they'll be after us, following us all over France."

"Ah, yes. I see it now," he said: "a close-up of Jean Gabin on his motorcycle. He's playing a cop in this one. He's also playing your father."

"Then there's a scene in a church," she said, "or a convent. The mother superior is leaning over me. 'Was that you I saw kneeling on the stairs, child?' she asks. 'On what stairs, Mother?' I ask. 'On the hotel stairs,' she says, and her eyes darken."

"Is she played by Monsieur Gabin too?" he asked.

"I don't know. Her face is hidden. Wait. No. Yes. It's you! You!!"

They laughed wildly. Having picked up speed, he was barely staying on the road now. After a while the laughter was behind them and they slowed down.

The morning passed and part of the afternoon. The sky lightened and darkened. At times it seemed as if it might rain again, at times as if it might snow. If he had been able to maintain any kind of speed, who knows where they might be by now? But they were only somewhere, somewhere driving on minor roads through abandoned fields. They would never arrive. They were not even in motion. Yet at times he had the illusion of a terrible backdrop in front of him: the road, the countryside, the sky itself, flat as a painting and coming to an end in about fifty yards, an absolute end coming up to meet him, fast. And he would flinch and the car with him.

"What is it?" she asked.

"Nothing."

"Did you see something?"

"No."

"I didn't either," she said.

The road began to rise, and as the country became rougher, there were more slowing twists and turns. The incline too slowed them, and the cold began to penetrate to them. Barely moving, the car was louder now, and still louder after every turn, shaking their tired bodies. The broken, valueless land, which was not scenery either, seemed to move closer to the road. The trees were suddenly too close together, shapeless. Great outcroppings of rock like dead factories surrounded them. Elsewhere the surface appeared to be subsiding, drawing the shadows in after the dank, rotting leaves, and darkening, the land seemed ready to close over them too. Where are we, where are we—he began to hear a voice within him, straining with the car. Why is the world so bleak? Why am I so tired? What's wrong?

Suddenly they seemed to emerge from the shadow of a crevice. They were on top of something and the rays of the sun, far away to the south, were upon them. But it was here on the top that the rain had fallen, or the dark wet clouds had preceded them. For they came to a stop suddenly in a forgotten forest of small old trees, and each tree, to the smallest distinct twig, had been brushed with clear, hard ice. Sparkling now in the light from the low, distant sun, the forest reflected a rainbow of color, tiny points of gently moving color, and as the branches touched each other they seemed to tinkle and ring in the softly moving, clear cold air.

They must have left the car and wandered in among the trees, the ground lightly crackling beneath their steps until they stopped somewhere and stood still, silent, included. The sun moved lower in the sky and time passed.

"Hey," she said. "Where are you?"

"I'm right here," he said, knocking his cold hands together.

"You were mumbling."

"I was?"

95

"You said 'Ah, ah, ah.' " He shook his head. "That's when I spoke up."

"Thank you," he said quietly. He looked around him then and it was all unfamiliar. Where was he? Where was he?

"Hey!"

"Hey, what?"

"Hey, you're in the ice forest," she said.

"Am I?"

"Yes, and you might never get out."

The sun touched the horizon and began to flatten. She had taken the front of his coat in her gloved hand and was shaking it gently. She laughed a little and he could see her breath.

"Will you lead me out?" he asked suddenly.

"Yes," she nodded. "I think I'd better drive too."

In the end he found the car first.